The Quest For
# An Eternity of Peace
In the Universe

**M.D.K**

# Contents

# Dedication

I dedicate this book to God and my loving family, who is brimming with love, and adventure; never a dull moment. Life is an amazing bumpy ride that I adore so much, and a shoutout to God's universe, galaxies and planets, and our loving mother Earth, filled with my beloved animal kingdom that I am so blessed to have a top shelf kinship with xoxo MDK.

# Acknowledgments

I acknowledge all of the many blessings I've been given from God's heaven and all the good, pure old souls around, my family and all my fans and the team of people who helped put everything together! Thank You!

# About the Author

Born in Winnipeg, Manitoba, Canada, on June 9, 1977. He Came to Calgary, Alberta, Canada, at the age of one. To call Calgary home. With his two lovely parents, Carole and Cornell and their beloved white, fluffy Persian cat named Pushue. He grew up with lots of reading and Christmas skiing trips to Whitefish, Montana, USA. He played lots of baseball and spent summers in Hawaii being at one/peace with the universe, praying, earthing, and surfing. He has always been very blessed with many things, one being having a super strong positive bond, a pure, true kinship with the animal kingdom. He has always enjoyed each day on God's green earth. A pure family of God's children. Well-rounded, hard-working and fun at family barbecues. Camping. Learning, and laughing each day. Always growing, evolving on God's team, doing his best.

# Foreword

After the devil/Lucifer went against God, he got his wings clipped. He never tried to make things right with God…always went against him, so now there are two teams. Team God and Team Satan. After all the sins and zero good deeds from team Satan towards God. He will take away any power that Satan has and take away the hell that he created for the devil from him and all of the devil's followers. Then, team Satan will be cast out of God's universe. Apart into darkness and separation forever and ever in the name of Jesus Christ,

*Amen*

# Part I

# Chapter: 1

The legacy of the quest began on Kozoway Island. When Chase and Hope awoke one glorious sunny day, they decided to indulge and relax in some tai chi and yoga together. The happily married couple had met each other when they were young, many moons ago. It was love at first sight. Chase took a wishbone out of his pocket and said to Hope, "Make a wish, and don't tell anyone what your wish is, whether you win or lose."

Chase asked, "Are you ready?" Hope replied, "Yes!"

"On three," Chase counted. "One… Two… Three!" They both tugged on the wishbone, and with a snap, the top piece flew off, landing in the sand. To their surprise, they were left holding equal halves—something almost unheard of. It meant both their wishes would come true. Smiling, they wrapped each other in a big, joyful bear hug.

Hope told Chase, "Let's go down to the beach and pray and swim with the dolphins."

The loving couple locked hands and started walking down the sandy path together. The path leads down to the beach and ocean. They said hello to some of the animals along the way that they shared the island with, like Maximus, the lion. Chase and Hope looked over at a nearby palm tree and said, "Good morning," to Skye, the bald eagle, and Lola, the turtle.

They walked down to the beach near the surf and sat down in the sand. They looked up to the heavens, then out to the big blue lady and the breathtaking Sun. A truly rare gem of synchronicity began. Hope and Chase are thankful for having each other "True Love" and are blessed with so many lovely gifts, such as their health and happiness. They both had an incredibly intense wave of joy and bliss wash over them. The hairs on the back of their necks began to stand up. Their hearts began to race as fast as hummingbirds. An enormous feeling of euphoria started inside of them. Feelings of pure love, peace, and comfort smashed into them like a meteor hit them. Goosebumps overtook their whole bodies from head to toe, and their eyes filled with tears. There were oh so vibrant Ora surrounded them with every bright color.

Chase and Hope opened their eyes. Tears were running down both of their faces. Both looked up at the sky. There was a magnificent cloud over them, and a rainbow started to emerge out of it and cast over Hope and Chase. The most beautiful set of big, lovely eyes and faces became predominant as the two were locked, staring into the deepest, mesmerizing eyes of all time. A heavy shower of gorgeous chains and pendants began to come down the rainbow (God's rainbow), landing in the sand at the feet of Chase and Hope. They were all the same solid gold, and glistening sparkling diamonds, and they formed the eternity symbol and a heart on the pendants. Chase picked them up, and they both stood up in the white sand simultaneously; Chase put one around his love's neck and then put one around his own.

Hope said to Chase, "I wonder 'who or 'what these other glorious gifts from God are for?"

Chase says, "I have a feeling that we're about to find out, pretty lady."

"Agreed", says Hope.

All of their senses were maxed out, like a race car redlining; sight, smell, touch, hearing, and physical abilities. The whole island was lit up with an electric array of every color. They looked up at the heavenly spirit's face filled with love. They both thanked Him, and Chase said, "We love you." "So much," said Hope. The cloud turned into the shape of the eternity symbol and the heart, the same as on the pendants. A small, soft sound of rustling came from deep in the island's core. They locked eyes with each other. Chase reached out for Hope's hand and locked his fingers with hers. The powerful, tropical sun glistened off their tanned skin, and the peaceful waves caressed their feet. Hope said, "I love you with all my heart and Soul, my handsome King."

"Right back at you, my stunning, heavenly Queen." Replied Chase. "Our love is forever."

There was a lot more scrambling coming from the shrubbery of the island. Magic was fully brewed up in the one-of-a-kind paradise. The old Souled couple shared this place with many animals.

Chase said, "It sounds like it's coming from God's Alpha Squad's Den." Hope and Chase both came from a long line of military families. They cherish wolves, they are loyal and family-oriented, and they mate for life. Both of their truly legendary family trees always did and always will believe in strength, honor, and loyalty. Chase even got all of the wolf pack 'dog tags' with "God's Alpha Squad" and each of their names on them. They wore these tags with all their pride. Sure enough, the thunder of many paws, claws, and heavy panting was drawing near. The first wolf that came out of the trees was Miles, the pack's leader—followed closely by his daughter Faith. Her best friend Jade emerged moments later, with the rest of the pack joining up, and they all enclosed around Hope and Chase. The rest of the necklaces and pendants were in the sand by their feet and paws. Things were very different now, even though there was a true connection and bold bond before. Chase reached out and patted Miles on his head. Miles traded the affection by jumping up on them and licking their faces.

Chase turned to Miles and asked, "How's life, my loyal brother?" Without moving his mouth, Miles responded, "Living large, and so are the others. Thanks for asking! How are you all?"

Hope, wide-eyed, gasped, "Did you just hear that?!"

Without missing a beat, Chase nodded. "Yes!"

They both realized they could now hear the animals' thoughts. Grinning, Chase replied, "That's amazing! We've never been better, and it's great to hear from our furry friends!"

Hope bent down and picked up three necklaces, and Chase picked up three more. They both placed the necklaces on all six of the wolves' necks. The pack thanked Hope and Chase, to which they happily replied, "You're all very welcome."

It seemed as though the animals of the land were the first to arrive out of the other two sea and air. Next down to the scene was Ozzy. Hope and Chase both called him head of security. He's an elite and wise fourteen-foot-tall Kodiak bear. With him came his two sidekicks, Scar, the grizzly bear, and Wreaker, the wolverine. Chase warmly greeted them and asked how they were. Ozzy said, "Wonderful! We were in our cave in hibernation slumber. I was the first to awake. We felt that undeniable positive wave of euphoria wash over us, and we were drawn to where we are standing with you now."

Chase smiles and approaches Ozzy with a necklace, which Ozzy lowers his massive head so he can place it over his head onto his neck. Hope gave the other two theirs.

Suddenly, a loud, strange stampeding noise was coming from beyond the treeline towards them. Realizing that all of the land animals on the island must have felt and heard what happened and were all heading down to the beach. The next animals to come were their beloved dog and cat, Mider and Perogy. They are beloved pets that mainly live in the castle with Hope and Chase. They love going on adventures with them or hunting around together for all hours of the night. All shapes and sizes were emerging. Maximus, the massive lion, was there with Lushis, the bangle tiger. Chika, the cheetah, and Jewel, the snow leopard. They were all purring as they joined the gathering.

Hope and Chase gave them all their necklaces. They noticed that no matter how big or small, once placed on their bestowed neck, they would magically adjust to every size to fit perfectly.

Lucky, the ladybug flew over and landed on Chase's shoulder. Chase said, "According to a legend, if a ladybug lands on you, it's Lucky." Hence, the couple agreed on how perfect Lucky is! It would always prove they were on the right path when she landed on them. Freeheart the Dragonfly came over with his Buddy Pal the Praying Mantis. These two always hung out together. Chase gave Lucky her necklace while Hope tossed two into the air. Freeheart and Pal flew through them just as they perfectly transformed around their necks. Coming out of the brush now was Wisdom the red fox, Ombre the raccoon, and Whiskey the weasel. These guys were always together, getting into good old-fashioned mischief and trouble. Raiding the chicken coops for eggs and things like that. Hope and Chase didn't mind, as it was part of their nature. Hope greeted them with a smile and presented them with their necklaces.

Next approached was the other castle mate, Packer, a beautiful Australian blue healer. He has his own dog house but prefers to stay in the castle. Chase gave him his, and then he jumped up and affectionately licked his face.

Suddenly, a loud crashing sound echoed through the trees, followed by the snapping of branches and heavy stomping. Stampers the elephant emerged, flanked by Knuckles the silverback gorilla, Boomerang the chimpanzee, Groosefraba the polar bear, Brooks the bison, Angel the arctic fox, and Sneak the king cobra. They were the last of the Land Pals, coming over to say hello and express their gratitude for the precious gifts.

Curious, they asked what was happening. Chase smiled and replied, "You're all very welcome, my friends. I know you must have many questions, but I think it's best to wait for the others, as I'm sure they'll be here soon."

Just as he finished speaking, a cawing sound came from the tops of the palm trees lining the beach. It was two of their feathered friends: Soul the crow and Loyal the raven. Only the Gods knew how long they had been perched there. Clover, the snowy owl, was also sitting on a nearby palm tree, gazing down at them with her large yellow eyes. These three were true overseers, often remaining silent as they quietly observed everything around them.

It was apparent that the friends of the sky were next on the scene. Hope threw three necklaces into the air, and they landed perfectly around their intended owners as they stayed perched. Then way, way, way up in the blue sky was Scoops the falcon, and Skye was the bald eagle. The rest of the members of the air. They both went into an intense dive bomb from a thousand feet up and were aimed straight at Chase! A few seconds later, they both landed and perched on his shoulders.

"Those were two breathtaking dive bombs both of you just did," Chase said as he gave them their necklaces. "Thanks," said Skye, "couldn't help it. So, what on God's green earth is going on here? The rainbow, the whole island is glowing, and everyone has an incredible aura around them, including myself." Chase grinned and said, "I know, my pal. It seems as though it's a wild and special day! I will do my best to explain it all to you. We are just waiting for everyone to arrive first." Scoops piped up and said he caught sight of Rip and our other sea dweller friends. Everyone looked out into the sea. Just off the horizon was Rip, the 30-foot great white shark; Kahara, the Orca whale; Tusk, the walrus; Destiny and Moon, the dolphins; and Tigerclaw, the otter. Tusk and Tigerclaw came up onto the beach. Hope met them with necklaces as Chase walked past another 20 ft into the surf where the last four were. They circled Chase as he passed out their necklaces. Chase patted Rip on his massive head, and the other three were swimming in a tight circle around him, splashing playfully.

He had a smile from ear to ear as he walked back to the beach. He paused and looked around the beach filled with all his animal friends. Reached for Hope's hand to hold and said loudly for all to hear, "Everyone, please listen up! Come gather round." They all came in closer; even the four in the sea came as close as they could.

Chase explained how Hope and he had spent their morning in the usual way with yoga and tai-chi. "We decided to break a wishbone together as we each made a wish, which broke into three pieces. I'm sure you all know what that means?"

Miles, head of God's Alpha Squad, spoke up first and said, "That means you both get what you wished for!"

Hope nodded and said, "Yes, Miles, so they say!"

Chase continued explaining how they decided to come to this spot and pray, which was where they both had their experience. Chase and Hope shared every detail of their magnificent and heavenly time. All of the animals oohed and awed, howled and meowed, and all the above. Everyone embraced in a true inner circle love embrace. The whole island shimmered with colours. Many of the animals hadn't seen one another in quite some time, between the Isle being so large and the lifestyles and sleeping patterns differing.

Chase said, "Our intense spiritual visitation from the Gods and Goddesses and the lovely gifts that we have all received is telling me that we have truly united clans even more so than we did before. We are all destined for a higher purpose, as individuals and as a group. I think we should live by our strength, honour, and loyalty to the absolute fullest and become ONE! If anyone has a problem with that, please speak now and please leave your necklace behind. I give my word that you may go in peace, and none of us will judge you, which should go without saying."

The lack of sound on the island made it very apparent no one wanted to leave. It was so quiet you couldn't even hear a mouse rustling in the grass, nor any of the many crickets that inhabited the island—pure and total peace.

"Well," Chase says, "Actions speak louder than words and all that good stuff. I see we are all in agreement, and it's not surprising. Hope, and I love and trust each of you. Everyone here has been on Kozoway Island for many years, and each has brought something to the table with great passion. Hope and I are so proud of all you fine beings."

Hope beamed from ear to ear, her joy mirrored by everyone else. Chase continued, "Our powerful feelings and vibrant auras are what brought us all together. Who's to say they haven't attracted others in the same way? Old friends, new friends, and even those with ill intentions?"

Ozzy the Kodiak stood up, nodding in agreement. "I was just thinking the same thing." Miles the wolf and Maximus the lion echoed his sentiments, along with many others.

"Exactly," Hope added. "We must stand tall as one!"

"Yes, united," said Ozzy. "Theory is important, but experience is paramount. There's a large stockpile of artillery hidden around the island—weapons passed down through Chase and Hope's family. It has always been their bloodline's priority to stay safe and be prepared to protect what's right: family, friends, and, if necessary, their island! We need to gather these weapons. Everyone, stay alert!

Chase and Hope, I want you to head up to the castle, collect whatever you need, and secure it. Then, make your way to the boats docked at the pier. Ensure they're stocked with plenty of food and weapons. I want the Gods' Alpha Squad to accompany you, keeping watch and helping carry supplies."

Chase replied, "That's a big ten-four, Ozzy!" Ozzy nodded and continued to take action and give out orders. "I want the rest of the land animals to stay together in equal groups on each of the four corners of the island. Rip the Great White, and the other sea creatures need to watch the ocean. Soul the crow and all of the other feathered friends need to keep watch on the sky and remember to rotate their watch. One from each group must be awake to keep watch and wait to be relieved from their shift. Scar and Wrecker will be with me, and don't forget to be safe; Ozzy loves you!"

Everyone shouted, "YES!"

# Chapter: 2

Chase thought riding Stampers up to the castle and down to the boats would be a great idea. Maximus the lion could tell what Chase was thinking and ran up to Chase as he climbed onto his back, and with a furious jump, Maximus made short work for the two, getting on top of the giant beast Stampers. They began to make their way up the sandy path. Maximus jumped off. Miles and the rest of the wolf pack were close behind. They quickly scurried across the beach and up the windy sandy path. Everything around them was more alive. A lot of the trees had faces if you looked. And now they all did.

As they reached the top of the path, a vast plateau stretched before them, dominated by towering trees—red oak, cherry, apple, lemon, lime, and walnut—all deeply rooted in the earth. Fresh food and water were never a concern on the island. A rare underground spring fed by a freshwater pocket beneath the sea rose through tunnels and caves, eventually forming a large pool in a hidden cavern. From there, the water cascaded down a mighty waterfall, branching into soothing streams and babbling brooks, with some flowing back into the sea.

The island was rich with resources: boat docks lined its shores, every kind of fruit and nut tree flourished, and massive fruit and vegetable gardens thrived alongside a vineyard producing fine wines. A barn and a trout pond offered a peaceful retreat for those looking to fish and relax.

Stampers had made the journey swiftly, pausing beside the ancient red oak. As Chase and Hope stood there, they noticed something unusual—a face formed in the bark, moving and staring right at them. Then it spoke, "Hello, my name is Sunset. It's a pleasure to finally meet you both, Hope and Chase."

Chase replied, "Likewise, my friend. I see you have watched over everything for many years and get to see the sun go down, hence your name. That's terrific."

Hope said, "We have had many picnics under you; it was lovely to have met you."

"Likewise," said Sunset.

Stampers continued running towards the castle. They picked up the pace to high gear, vastly approaching the moat that was all around the castle. That's where Stone the Crocodile and fellow Crocs lived. Stone prided himself on never leaving his post; he loved his home. Chase said, "I bet he's still there." They continued and were coming up and over a small grass knoll with tropical flowers. They came to the foot of the drawbridge, all looking down; sure enough, there was stone…staring up at them …all smiled. This way is one of three ways to get in and out of their home. Another being a helicopter that's on the roof…a door up there. And a series of underground caves that lead inside and go to the Gondola and Ozzy the bear's den. They also lead to each corner of the island and one to the boat dock. Stampers extended his trunk, and the couple both got on; he lowered them down to the ground. Chase had set up a secret way to get the drawbridge up and down.

As they approached the two water fountains on either side, Chase noticed the sculptures: Cupid, armed with his bow and arrows, carved from stone, and an angel holding a heart. Their eyes suddenly seemed to come to life. Both statues winked at Chase, and he winked back with a grin. Traditionally, those who knew the secret would pull down on Cupid's right wing, triggering him to shoot an arrow into the heart held by the angel. But this time, something was different. The statues, whose eyes had always appeared to follow people, were fully alive, moving and greeting everyone.

Chase reached out to trigger Cupid's wing, but before he could, Cupid beat him to it, shooting an arrow directly into the heart. The bridge immediately lowered to their feet. Hope smiled and thanked Cupid, and the angel returned her smile. They walked to the middle of the bridge and peered down at the moat. Sure enough, Stone was there, staring up at them, already wearing his necklace. It was as if the powers that be had anticipated that Stone wouldn't leave for the beach and had bestowed his gift on him early. Naturally, Stone asked what was going on, and Miles quickly filled him in.

As this was happening, Chase pointed upward at the gargoyle statues that adorned the top of the castle. Gargoyles were scattered across the island, and in many cultures, they were revered as protectors, warding off evil. Hope looked up, followed by the others, and gasped, "Oh my, that's incredible!" Like the Cupid and angel statues, the gargoyles were alive and watching them. Hope waved with a warm smile, and all seven gargoyles they could see waved back—using their wings!

Soul, the crow, perched atop the center gargoyle, watching over everything. "Look up at the sky!" Hope exclaimed. High above them, they spotted Scoops the falcon and Skye the eagle, circling together, keeping a vigilant eye on everything below. Their vision was sharp enough to spot a fish in the sea or a mouse in the grass from miles up.

Chase then noticed the opera music streaming from the castle windows, louder than before. "Everything feels enlightened!" he marveled. "You didn't turn up the music, did you, my love?" Hope shook her head, smiling. At that moment, Skye let out three loud screeches from the clouds above. They all looked up in response. Soul echoed the call with three sharp caws, before swooping down and landing gracefully on Hope's shoulder. "There's a mist approaching from the roof," he warned. "It feels warm and positive, but let's stay alert."

Hope, ever prepared, twirled two harmony balls from the Orient in her right hand while clutching healing crystals in her left. She put the balls away and pulled out some native sweetgrass, lighting it with her grandfather's lucky matches. The mist began creeping over the roof, cascading down the walls and vines. It was thick, shimmering with the iridescent colors of an oyster—glowing whites and purples.

Miles and Faith, two of the wolves, growled softly, their fangs bared, as the mist descended on either side of Hope. "Calm down, my family," she soothed. "It's warm and positive!" Jade and the other wolves gathered around, on edge, eyes wide, fur standing on end. A wave of goosebumps rippled through them all as the mist enveloped them. Chase reassured everyone, "This is a joy-filled friend, like a fine Italian wine!"

The mist now descended over the drawbridge and Stampers head, he smiled and raised his head high in the air, trumpeting loudly. Mider, the Jack Russell Terrier, and Perogy, the grey cat, dashed out from behind a bush, rubbing affectionately against Chase's legs. The mist covered them all, exuding a sense of peaceful energy, stronger even than the sweetgrass. The smoke from Hope's burning sweetgrass began to glow, forming shapes—hearts of different sizes—and everyone rejoiced. Meows and howls filled the air as they all felt rejuvenated and invincible.

"This is remarkable!" Hope exclaimed, noticing that their necklaces and pendants were glowing even more brightly. Meanwhile, the magical mist had spread across the island, blanketing everything in a protective embrace. Chase took Hope's hand, and they walked toward their home, Stampers following close behind—there was plenty of space for even an elephant in the castle. The mist seemed to rise from the basement, flowing through the home and out the roof.

Chase approached the massive fireplace, where a few large logs still burned from the magical full-moon night. He smiled, mesmerized by the flickering flames, which danced in the shape of hearts, their colors vibrant and hypnotic. He reached up to press down on the angel's halo, which triggered the drawbridge to rise, but the angel smiled at him and did the work herself. Chase smiled back and thanked her.

He stepped back to a favorite spot, where he and Hope loved to relax, and admired the painting of the handsome couple above the fireplace. On either side of the room stood two enormous 5,000-gallon saltwater fish tanks, teeming with marine life—sharks, puffer fish, lionfish, seahorses, and more. The peacefulness of the moment was beyond words as the fish swam up to the glass to greet them.

Suddenly, there was a loud bump and scratching at the drawbridge. Faith and Miles dashed over, curious. It was Ozzy, Scar, and Wrecker, sliding down the bridge at breakneck speed. Chase rushed over but almost got bowled over by the three, who tumbled onto the stone floor, laughing. The heavy drawbridge closed behind them with authority. "We heard Skye's call, and then Soul," Ozzy said, pausing to breathe. "This mist... it feels amazing!"

Everyone nodded in agreement. "We saw it covering all of you," Ozzy continued. "We ran right through it, and I feel reborn!" Scar and Wrecker echoed his sentiments.

Hope smiled and looked around. "Could this day get any more fanhevenlytastic?" she wondered aloud.

Glad to see everyone is safe said, Ozzy.

Hope said to Chase, "Let's go down to the basement to see where this mist is coming from?"

"Absolutely," Chase said. "Okay, Hope you, God's Alpha Squad, and myself will take the elevator. And Ozzy, Scar, and Wrecker, you three take the spiral stairs. Both of these ways lead from the top to the bottom of their home. Along with three secret passageways that were all connected. Ranging from walls that slid back and forth to fireplaces, pool table, and an old past-down grandfather clock!"

Both of the couple's family trees adored mystery! And keeping some things to themselves and being creative, to say the least! Miles ran over to the elevator and pressed the down arrow with his paw. Door opened!

Miles said, "It's here. Let's go!"

All got on. Ozzy and his sidekicks ran towards the spiral stairs; Ozzy waited for the door of the elevator to close before they went down… Chase said to Stampers,

"Do you remember how to trigger the drawbridge if you need to get out?"

Stampers said, "Yes, my family, I love you!"

Hope said, "We love you too!"

The door closes. Ozzy and the other two started running down the stone steps. It is one hundred feet from the main floor living room to the basement. Soul the crow flew through one of the tiny stained glass windows that was open, with three iron bars through it. Hope left it open when they were enjoying the breakfast that Chase cooked.

Meanwhile, the elevator reached the basement, the door opened up. They all got off. The other three reached the bottom of the steps at the same time. Chase and Hope both had stashes of weapons, food, and water throughout Kozoway castle and the island. But the main concentration of the three, mixed together in a fire, waterproof boxes, and duffle bags with locks, were in the basement. The couple both grabbed half the stockpile of each box and bag at a time and dispensed them equally to everyone.

Ozzy said with a smirk, "You can never be too safe! Feels like we should be prepared for anything!!"

Just then, they all heard…

"Chase! Hope!" In a raspy voice… then… Cacao! Cacao! That of Soul, the crow! He was mid-souring down the spiral stone stairs. Then, he flew through to the bottom and perched up on Chase's shoulder. Then some sounds of pitter! Patter! Of paws and claws against the stone… nearing… and out popped Mider and Perogy! Mider said, "Count us in too!"

Soul said, "I just spotted a helicopter and a boat. Both are filled with men and women! Headed towards the marina and the main watch tower! The one at the highest part of the island."

"Okay," said Miles, "thank you, Soul!"

"Always," he replied.

"Okay," Ozzy spoke up, "let me quarterback this! It's the same thing; you guys take the elevator with supplies, and we will take the stairs. But this time, Soul, you fly ahead of us double time and try and let me know what's going on before we all reach the top."

They all boarded the elevator, and the mist that was coming up from the basement floor started to go up the stairs in a thicker, faster manner.

Soul called out, "See you at the top." As he started to fly off ahead of the group.

Ozzy and the crew started off in an aggressive scamper up the steps. Before long, the three notice each step further than one of their normal strides. The mysterious mist had swept them up and lifted them up at a furious pace. Only seconds passed, and they soared past Soul, who was almost at the top. Out and at the top of the lookout point. Ozzy looked over at the strange mist that was settling all around their feet. He stared a bit longer and decided to say, "Thank you, my friend." Then he gazed out over the ocean to where the noise was all about, noticing the helicopter and boat were nearly at the Island's edge.

"You two! Go check on the others, NOW!" Ozzy shouted.

Wrecker looked over and said, "The doors were still closed; we must have gotten here oh so fast!"

That's when the upward arrow on the elevator lit up, and after a few seconds passed, the doors opened, and everyone piled out of the elevator and went over to the edge of the tower.

Chase announced that these were the people from the closest island. Chase has met them a few times in the past, sharing some of the same sky and sea. This time, the aura's around them are even darker. A glow of charcoals and blackness swirled around them.

Ozzy asked, "Do you think they saw the clouds, rainbows, and mist?" Most of the animals on the island had gathered near the harbor, where strangers approached by both land and sea. As they drew closer, the animals huddled together, except for Soul, who swooped down from the sky. The island had a gondola system that ran to the edge of the bay, where yachts, speedboats, and jet skis were docked. The strangers were using it to transport supplies, heading towards the shore.

Soul perched stealthily on the last pier post, where the ocean waves crashed violently, spraying saltwater across his feathers. He watched the sea intently, squawking loudly as the strangers' boat came within 700 feet of the shore. His calls grew louder, attracting attention. Just as the gondola arrived and its doors opened, the rest of the group, led by Chase, disembarked. They looked curiously at the bubbles forming in the water near the harbor's entrance, swirling unnaturally. Chase asked, "Has anyone ever seen bubbles like these before?" Everyone shook their heads, puzzled.

The island's animals, from land to sky, began to gather around the harbor. Lucky the ladybug fluttered over from a nearby palm tree, landing on Hope's shoulder. "I figured you could use all the luck you can get," she said cheerfully. "Thank you, darling," Hope replied with a smile. Soon after, Freeheart the dragonfly swooped down, carrying his friend, a praying mantis, on his back. Together, they began flying in the shape of an infinity symbol above the group's heads, joined by the other birds circling overhead.

Above, the deafening sound of helicopter blades echoed across the island. Even Jake, the jackrabbit, removed his headphones—customarily tuned to Sir Elton John—due to the intense noise. The chopper landed roughly on the beach, kicking up sand and debris. The pilot cut the engine, and the blades slowly came to a halt.

At the mouth of the harbor, the yacht, now anchored, was suspiciously close to the swirling bubbles. Onboard, three men and three women, all dressed in black with holstered handguns, stepped forward. Tension grew as God's Alpha Squad, the island's protector animals, surrounded Hope and Chase, growling and staring down the intruders.

The captain of the yacht called out, "Ahoy there! We don't mean to intrude!" Chase, his voice firm, replied, "This is a private island. What brings you here?" The captain pointed toward the southern horizon. "We're your closest neighbors, from the island over yonder. We noticed some unusual clouds and a rainbow. What's going on here?"

Before anyone could respond, the water erupted in a violent swirl. A massive red tentacle, covered in razor-sharp hooks, shot out from beneath the surface. Ozzy recognized it immediately. "That's Thorn! He's a kind soul but fiercely protective. Something must be wrong with these strangers. Thorn only appears when evil is near."

More tentacles emerged, towering above the yacht and the helicopter. Without warning, Thorn's tentacles lashed down, grabbing the four strangers on the beach, squeezing them tightly before dropping them harshly onto the sand. The four, gasping for breath, scrambled toward the chopper in panic. Thorn's massive tentacles then wrapped around the yacht, crushing it into splinters in a matter of seconds. His final tentacle hovered ominously above the helicopter.

Ozzy shouted, "Are you going to kill them, Thorn?"

Thorn's deep voice echoed from the water. "No, I've only given them a scare. But next time, I won't be so nice."

Miles, one of the wolves, stepped forward. "Thank you, my friend. I can tell they're bad people. Their energy feels dark, evil."

As Thorn's tentacles withdrew, the strangers scrambled into the helicopter, their heads bowed, avoiding eye contact with anyone. Without uttering a single word, the chopper lifted off, its engine revving to full throttle. No one looked back as the helicopter sped away, disappearing into the tropical sunset.

"Good riddance," said Miles, his voice filled with satisfaction. "Here, here," added Chase, as the group cheered.

Thorn's voice rumbled once more from the depths. "I've been watching those people for a while now. They're always up to no good, arguing and scheming. Today, they were planning to take over this island. When they saw the mist and clouds, they rushed over to investigate."

Hope looked out at the horizon, the danger now passed, and smiled. "Well, they won't be coming back anytime soon." The animals roared, howled, chirped, and meowed in agreement as peace settled once again over the island.

# Chapter: 3

A perfect white, fluffy cloud began to glow brightly above the gathering. Its ethereal light bathed the entire island in a serene, heavenly glow, capturing the attention of Chase, Hope, and all the animals present. They instinctively turned their eyes skyward, watching in awe as something emerged from the radiant cloud. Slowly descending, shimmering like a falling star, another necklace—its pendant gleaming with an otherworldly brilliance—floated down and gently landed around Thorn's neck, the wolf who had been striving for redemption.

Miles, the leader of the wolves, who had long watched Thorn's journey with careful eyes, stepped forward. His deep voice reverberated through the clearing as he said, "Now we will see if he's truly good, for it is known: if one's heart is impure, the pendant will turn black and fall away." The crowd hushed, holding their collective breath as they awaited the revelation.

Thorn's aura, once subdued and uncertain, began to shimmer with a kaleidoscope of vibrant colors—yellows, oranges, purples—dancing around him like the northern lights. Hope gasped, her hand flying to her mouth. "Look!" she exclaimed, her voice filled with wonder. "The chain! It's glowing… staying golden!"

Miles nodded, a proud smile tugging at the corner of his mouth. "Welcome, brother," he said, his tone warm and filled with acceptance. "Kozoway Island is now your home, too. You are one of us—a member of our family." His words echoed with deep meaning, and as he spoke, the other animals stirred with approval, nodding and murmuring their agreement. Thorn, overcome with emotion, stepped forward, his heart swelling with newfound purpose and pride.

"Thank you, brother Miles, and to all my new brothers and sisters!" Thorn's voice was strong but carried the weight of deep gratitude. "I feel… incredible. I am at home, truly. I accept this honor—the powers and blessings you've bestowed upon me—with all my heart and soul. I pledge to stay loyal, forever, to protect this sacred land and our family."

The animals around him, a magnificent blend of wolves, lions, birds, and creatures of the land and sky, cheered in unison. Their voices, howls, and roars rose into the heavens, filling the island with an overwhelming sense of unity and purpose. Thorn's heart pulsed with the collective strength of his newfound family. Chase, the leader of their alliance, stepped forward, his eyes glinting with the fire of determination.

"We are there for you anytime, Thorn," Chase declared, his voice carrying the weight of a leader's promise. "We will always stand by your side, brother."

The animals erupted in another wave of cheers, their morale soaring to its peak. The sheer energy of their collective spirit caused the very ground beneath them to hum with power. Chase raised his hand for silence, his eyes scanning the crowd with a seriousness that settled them all.

"Listen, everyone!" Chase began, his tone more solemn now. "Those who sought to harm us before… they may come back, and this time, they might not be alone. They may bring others who would wish to battle us here, on our own land!"

"Here! Here!" roared Maximus, the lion, his mighty voice filled with righteous fury. His roar was followed by Soul, the crow, who croaked, "I second that!" Their resolve was infectious, and once again, the island's inhabitants burst into cheers of defiance.

Hope, her spirit glowing as brightly as her golden necklace, stepped forward and raised her voice. "We must protect everything that is sacred here—God's power, the blessings of the spirits, and the angels that watch over us. Our home must remain ours, safe from the reach of evil."

Miles, always the voice of wisdom, nodded gravely. "It seems we've been united for a higher purpose," he said, his eyes gleaming with certainty. "To guard this land for the greater good, empowered by the light—the most powerful force in the universe."

All those present nodded in agreement, their hearts resonating with his words. Just then, as if in response to their unity, letters began to form in the sky, swirling out of the fluffy white clouds like divine messages. The crowd watched, mesmerized, as the letters came together in words that filled the blue sky above:

"Chase, Hope, and all the family of Kozoway Island, there is great need for your help to heal and restore this perfect planet I have created for all good souls. From the tropical islands to the mango groves, from the roses to the seas and mountains, paradise is within your reach. The sky is not the limit; there are no limits. Never quit, never give up. Keep your spirits high. There are quests you must complete, each one vital. Stand against the wrong and evil that seeks to claim power. Good luck. I will always believe in you. Bless you all."

The words lingered for a moment, glowing in the sky before they began to dissolve into the bright blue once more, leaving only their powerful message behind. The animals stood still, absorbing the enormity of the task laid before them.

Miles broke the silence, his voice filled with a sense of duty. "We must work together, as one, to fulfill this quest from start to finish. There's much to do."

Walking over to Chase and Hope, he placed a strong paw on Chase's shoulder, while Soul the crow swooped down and perched on his other, his sharp eyes gleaming with readiness. "We are ready," Miles declared. "Together, we will conquer whatever challenges come our way."

Suddenly, a rush of energy swept through them all, from their heads to their toes. Their jewels—the pendants that hung around their necks—began to glow with an intense brightness. Diamonds sparkled with renewed brilliance, casting radiant beams of light that connected them all in a web of shared power.

"|We're ready for anything!" Miles howled, his voice filled with anticipation and confidence. The others smiled and nodded, their spirits buoyed by the energy surrounding them.

"We need to start by investigating the island nearby," Chase said, his tone decisive. "We need to know what's happening over there."

Miles agreed with a firm nod. "Yes, and I'd like you, Hope, to take the chopper. Pick a few family members to accompany you."

Hope's eyes lit up. "I'll take God's Alpha Squad, Soul the crow, and Ozzy the Kodiak bear," she replied confidently.

Chase grinned. "Excellent choices! As for me, I'll take Groosefraba the polar bear—named in honor of the Eskimo elders—and Wisdom the fox, Umbra the raccoon, and Whiskey the weasel. We'll take the speedboat and follow you there."

He paused, looking over the gathered family. "I want half of our family, both land, air and sea, to stay here and defend Kozoway Island. The rest will join us on this mission."

At that moment, Lucky, the golden-eyed ladybug, fluttered over to Hope and perched on her shoulder. "I'm coming with you, Hope," she whispered, her voice soft but filled with power. "I pass my gift of luck to you and all our family. May it protect you forever, and ever." Hope gazed into Lucky's glowing eyes, feeling a warmth spread through her heart. Butterflies fluttered in her stomach, and a wave of love washed over her.

Chase, noticing the change in Hope, chuckled softly. "Well, now you're glowing gold just like Lucky!"

Everyone laughed, even Miles, whose usual stoic demeanor gave way to a rare smile. "Lucky, you've outdone yourself this time," Miles boomed in appreciation. "We are truly blessed to have you."

The energy in the air shifted, becoming lighter, more joyful. All around the island, the animals began to glow, their jewels sparkling with the gift of luck that Lucky had bestowed. Scoops the falcon and Skye the eagle soared above them, their wings catching the golden light, shimmering as they flew higher and higher.

As the joyous moment settled, Chase's voice cut through the air with a practical thought. "Before we set off, how about we fill our bellies? A hearty meal before a great quest is always wise."

Miles, ever the leader, barked out, "A feast! We'll celebrate this moment with a last supper before our adventure begins!"

Everyone cheered again, their hearts filled with excitement and camaraderie. As they began to prepare for the meal, Chase approached a nearby bonfire pit, intending to start a fire. But as he reached for the hatchet lying on the ground, something extraordinary happened—the hatchet floated up, straight into his hand.

The crowd gasped in astonishment. "Did you all see that?" Chase exclaimed, eyes wide with wonder. Miles laughed heartily. "You've unlocked a new gift, brother!"

With a smile of determination, Chase focused on the task at hand. Using nothing but his mind, he moved the hatchet toward a pile of logs. One by one, the logs split as if by magic, creating the perfect kindling for the bonfire. The crowd chanted his name in unison, "Chase! Chase! Chase!" The atmosphere was electric, filled with the anticipation of their upcoming journey.

As the fire roared to life, ignited by a lighter that floated of its own accord, Chase grinned. They were ready—ready for the quest, ready for the challenges ahead, and most of all, ready to defend the paradise they called home.

He moves it back over, it goes into place, and he buttons it down! Hands-free!! He carefully leaned over, moving a few logs onto the fire, cautious not to smother his handiwork. Looking up at Hope, he grinned and said, "See? Much easier to make a fire this way!" He chuckled, then let out a sigh, his shoulders slumping a bit. "Whew! My mind feels a bit tired after that! Guess I'll have to practice—practice makes perfect, right?"

Just then, a group of animals appeared, each bringing stacks of wood, enough for a bonfire that could last for days. The sun was beginning to set, painting the sky in warm tones as dusk settled around them. Miles had slipped away to the castle and returned with their favorite gold goblets from the kitchen—the ones he, Hope, and Chase loved to use on special occasions.

Soul, perched on Hope's shoulder, flew over to Miles, grasping a goblet in each set of talons. He brought one first to Hope and then to Chase, who both murmured their thanks. Wisdom, the fox, darted off to the wine cellar, while Umbra and Whiskey trotted toward the nearby yacht, returning with cases of island water, red and white wine, rum, and whiskey.

Chase picked up a familiar bottle of red wine—the one they'd shared on their third date all those years ago. He noticed the wax on the cork, cracked from age and memories. Just as they all looked on, the cork gave a final creak and burst free with a pop!

He then moved it snuggly close to his true love's goblet; she tilted it at a slight slant. And he kindly pored it much generously to the top. Then, he did the same for himself. Hope said thank you, my love! Now that's service!!, All laughed, and she gave him a huge hug! They put their gobbets of wine together. And Chase said a toast! To peace, true love, and being blessed wealthy in our hearts! And our gifts from God! At the time, he gave thanks to the family trees, and all of the members of the family passed away and the ones living amongst them. And a tribute, of course, to their God's gift of Kozoway Island and castle. In which many of the family trees, fruits of labours, mind, body and spirits, hard work and devotion all had a look up to God in heaven and said thank you, then Chase quickly glanced at all gathered, then the cases of water, wines, brandy, rums, champagne, … the wood tops flew off!! And he tossed them on the fire!! Then he used his power to float the bottles and gently scattered them in front of the family! He then said, please bear with me… I have a great thought!, he then started thinking of a freshly watered waterfall that was behind the castle, And strongly thought about making a stream of it come down to them. He pictured it from A to Z!, From start to finish. A trickling noise started to be apparent! And some garaging!! All stopped what they were doing,… and looked up at the crest of the hill above them! A steady stream of that tasty, quenching, bubbly water started making its way down to them. Gushing a new creek path, some going over Ozzy's paws! Then the lions and the wolves! All were lifting up their paws, They all began to lick them. The water then began to form a pool in the short grass beside the beach. All came over to enjoy a long lap, Drink of it! All that were holding bottles. The corks started flying off left, right, and center!! Chase had to sit down in the chair again! Wow! He said. That felt good!!! Cheers everyone!!! All had a drink together. Others had just brought down a fantastic feast of fresh fish, seaweed and rice wraps, fruits, and vegetables, just to name a few, to eat raw and to cook on the fire and immensely enjoy together. Chase said I almost can't believe I just made that stream!!?, But there it is, replied Miles!! All the bottles that he had hanging in mid-air were sagging a bite once he said that out loud! He realized that belief is half the battle! I do believe he shouted!! That I did that and kept doing it!! As he was saying that, the stream grew larger! And the bottles floated higher! A feast and celebration for all!! My family!!!! Hope then let out a sneeze! Chase said bless you, fancy face!! Then Miles said God bless the food and drinks we are about to receive!! All bowed their heads for a minute of thanks and respect for the big guy upstairs. And some even put together the first of the lobster, Crab, fish, and other yummy treats on a plate for God, and a glass of red wine and another of the island water to enjoy. With them, pure, honest respect is always shown. And if Jesus and the good side wanted to share in this fine five-star feast!!! Then so be it!! They all ate! ate! ate! And drank!drank!drank!drank!drank!and some even ate and drank some more!!! All heart's content!!! Chase kept up his newfound talent, Bringing bites of food, and sips of wine up to Hopes lushes lips! With only his eyes!!! Hope burst out laughing!! O Chase! I couldn't eat another bite! I adore and love it, though, my handsome king! Both smiled and giggled,... very contagious cackles all about! The family is pure bliss! United!! Sure, you're full; he bought up a giant prawn cooked golden brown, dripping in butter and sea salt. Garlic and a dash of white wine! She said that looks so scrumptious!! Okay, just this one more! How could I resist that!? Let's share it!! She took a big bite! And said that's beyond perfection!! She gave it to Chase and Miles to share. Some of the animals had made cups from coconuts and were sharing, like the birds, Soul, loyal, scoops, and Skye. Had tied a Vine from a palm tree to a palm tree. And hung up their cups. And all the sea and land lovers cackle laughs coming from deep in the hearts of story times from childhood! Scar the great white shark, Lola the turtle, Miles, and Ozzy are chatting about how much of an apple orange difference it's been since they awoke this morning to now!

Night had fallen, casting a serene glow over the island as it lit up below. Miles spoke up, his voice filled with gratitude and purpose, "What a journey we've already had! Sometimes, to reach true peace, you must be willing to stand up for yourself—finding that balance of inner strength and self-worth, and always keeping in mind the greater good for those who share the same positive goals." Everyone nodded in agreement, and conversation turned to the reality that sometimes, in the fight for good, tough choices had to be made. They knew that in order to achieve their quest for peace, they might have to confront darkness head-on.

Just then, their loyal friends appeared—Chase and Hope's beloved dog, Mider, and their cat, Perogy, who came rushing in with a bark and a meow. Mider announced with enthusiasm, "We want to take a boat out to the island. Perogy and I have been on countless adventures; we know how to run a boat!"

Chase chuckled, filled with pride at their courage. "With such confidence, I gladly give my blessing," he said. "The request is granted!" Miles turned to Mider, "So, who will you bring aboard?"

Mider responded eagerly, "We'll take Wrecker the Wolverine, Lushis the Tiger, and Chika the Cheetah." Perogy chimed in, "And we'll also bring Vine the Snake and Brooks the Bison."

Miles, smiling, added, "We have room for more. Any other volunteers?" Immediately, paws, claws, wings, and fins shot up in the air.

"Excellent! Let's gather a few from the sea and air to help us prepare the chopper and boats," Miles declared. "Bring enough food, water, and supplies—along with any weapons and ammo. We don't know what lies ahead or how long this mission will take. Be prepared, and stay on guard!"

Everyone gave a firm nod, their resolve unwavering. The quest for peace was about to begin.

Chase said we would leave at dawn. Some may need sleep. And others not!! He let out a loud cackle chuckle! But after we are ready and before anyone slumbers, I wish we all partake in the dance of the Donta!! Donta!! This is a very old dance that both sides of the family trees (Chase and Hope's) created and enjoyed! A cleanse to rid negative, nasty things! And bring positive energy and luck to the family and those in their lives! And cast away negative! It is pretty basic, though! All formed a circle around the fire and locked hands and paws… dancing around the blaze, saying Donta! Donta! And others were saying Donta means Donta!! Hahaha!! Funny and happy!! To say the least! All very much enjoyed this dance!! Quit the site, to see a bunch of humans, fur friends, and such. All holding hands, paws… doing a dance! Hope said I keep thinking of Stampers! She asks Chase when's the last time you saw him? In the castle? He knotted yes! Yeah, me too! I keep thinking of him, but not like normal, Seems much stronger! I'm drawn to him!!, I keep seeing him in my mind!! And he's on the bearskin rug in front of a roaring fire! On his back, legs up!! She chucked!! He's in a deep slumber; He seems to be really enjoying himself!! A tingle started to go over her whole body! And the image of Stampers got a lot more real! … in the flesh looking!! Incredibly vivid!! Her sight really began to focus on his eyes, the right pupil, to be precise! Getting tunnel vision …drawn into it! , till she was looking right up against it. Then her view clicked into something new! She could now see what he was dreaming about! He is in one of the tall grass fields of Kozoway Island with his family, mum, dad, and sister. Which he had not seen in a while; they had sadly passed away and had gone to the afterlife, Spirit side.

They all had long, lovely lives. Stampers had the gift of some sort of fountain of youth. Chase has it almost figured out in the lab to share his gift with the family. The last time they baked him a cake, it had five hundred candles on it! That was nearly a year ago. Hope spoke out and said Stampers! Stampers!! Stampers!!! He said yes, Hope!? I've known that voice for a long time!! But I don't see you. She chuckled, I don't know. I got a vision of you in the castle; now I can see you! I do feel like I'm being watched, to tell the truth! He starts looking around his whole dream- vision. Nothing, hmmmmm, I can't see you Hope? But it feels like you're watching from above. I can see you from above! Your family is over there with you, watching the sun just finishing setting. With a perfect picnic! Sooooo! Pretty!! All love! Bet this is your favorite dream! You bet your boots said the elephant. Breathtaking!! You're very Lucky to have such a family! Hope says you have slept through everything that's going on!! Not sure, he said. I was having very real-looking dreams of these gold and diamond Jewels falling from the heavens. God's eyes are staring down! There's no way I could explain or put it into words! How mesmerising and divine perfection it was, my dearest pal, Hope! All this glowing mist and all of our family of Kozoway Island coming together, some I had not seen in many, many years! There was a huge celebration and a bonfire, everyone was doing the dance of the Donta! Donta! And tons and tons of really yummy food! It made me so hungry! Watching my family picnic right after made me want to dance! Hope burst out laughing. Wow! Two w''s one o! Stampers, my old pal, you've pretty much got a dead-center bull's eye there! Heavy stuff, so what's going on? Well, there's lots going on, said Hope, I'll get you up to speed. We are all down at the beach having a celebration, a bonfire feast. Come down here; so much food and drinks! Of course I will, he said. Hope started to think over and over to get him to the feast. Chase came up to her and, in a muffled version of his voice, asked, Hope, are you okay? You seem extremely focused. On something? Gassing away! She put her right hand up and, without breaking focus on Stampers, put her thumb up! Chase then went back to chatting with Groosefraba, the polar bear. Hope was gazing off at a homemade heart loveseat that they had made out of willow. No one happened to be sitting on it at the moment. A small white star began to show itself! Getting bigger and bigger! Brighter and brighter!! On the heart-shaped piece that she was so intrigued with, Stampers said, I can see a star! Same here said Hope. An electric wave of a warm rush comes over her whole body! She goes back to see his eye; there is a small white star in his pupil! And flash!!! Pop!!! Stampers appeared in the loveseat!!! Just having time to get a leg down before smashing it to splinters! Miles yelled out abra cadabera! What just happened? He was still in the castle!?

Hope snapped out of her trance, her eyes bright with excitement. "Yes!" she exclaimed. "I was just in his dream, talking with him! It was amazing, to say the least!" Everyone burst into cheers, celebrating with shouts of "Stampers!" as he materialized before them.

"It seems I have a new power now, too!" Hope marveled. Just then, Groosefraba, one of the wisest Souls around, stepped up to give her a warm, comforting hug. Miles, Chase, and the others echoed the feeling, expressing how blessed and unstoppable all the good Souls of the universe truly felt.

Groosefraba returned with a tray of freshly smoked salmon on crackers topped with cream cheese, perfect for Hope and Stampers to share. Raising their glasses, they toasted to life. "Here, here!" cheered Thorn, the giant squid, lifting a massive arm from the surf and sending a playful splash everywhere. With a hearty laugh, he raised a keg of rum. "Cheers, all!"

Everyone took a sip of their drink, joining in the celebration. Then Chase called out, "Alright, anyone coming on the boats or the chopper, make sure to finish up any last-minute packing…is there anything else we might need?"

Miles dashed down the beach, wading into the surf as Thorn extended a giant arm. Hopping onto it, Miles ran across to another arm stretched out to the boat, eager to check if they were fully stocked with food and, of course, plenty of rum.

# Chapter: 4

Hope says ok, it will take us about thirty minutes to get over there by boat. We want to park the chopper on one of the landing pads both boats have. And come in slow! Chase gets in the chopper, starts it up, flies it over, and parks it on the one Miles is on. Miles starts sniffing the air! He goes to the chair where Chase is sitting; he starts scratching underneath the seat, more rustling. The sounds of a wolf's jaw opening and snapping shut, And Miles' face emerged with a bag of beef jerky in his fangs!

Out of the corner of his mouth, he said this is that homemade batch we made before our last hunting and fishing trip to the mainland! He then dropped it on Chase's lap. Wasting no time, he opened it and said o boy!! One of our best batches! They split it and ate it up happily. Miles said, Still chewing, and what a trip it was! Almost more wild game meat and fish than we could eat and bring home! Hope speaks up; it's going to be light out in an hour. Let's leave in a few minutes. I'd much rather start this by getting a view of the island at night. Ozzy the Kodiak bear says well said! I've packed night vision binoculars in both vessels, and most of us can sneak in under the cover of night… more of an advantage for us.

Most of them already had a funny little feeling in their guts; they were up to no good there. One must see for themselves, though. But never the less, always listen to your gut!! Your Soul bunches up there and tells you if it's good or bad! Depending on the type of tingling in your tummy! Positive or negative. Life gives us so many tools in our skill set to work with! One's insight can be limitless, depending on the Soul. Chase and Miles finished tying down the chopper.

Chase then went down inside the boat and fired up the engine. Mider and Perogy went in theirs and started it up. All of the crew that was going got on quickly. All ropes untied from the dock, and both boats set off. All saying goodbye! Chase says love you all, take care of yourselves and the island. Soul and loyal can fly over information, and or I'll be in touch with our satellite phones. I left another one in my office in the castle.

A few seconds after that, those on Kozoway Island could only see two small silhouettes in the light of the sea from the full moon. Maximus, the lion, stayed behind. He picked up a set of night binos that Chase left on the chair. He put them up to his natural night vision eyes; holy mackerel!! These make everything look like daylight! To a cat, anyway!! He giggled, And smiled; Scoops, the hawk flew over and landed on his shoulder and fluffy fury Maine. Our great king of the jungle! Let me have a look…. Scoops says very neat!! It looks only black and green to me, No cat vision, I can see them, though! What man makes sometimes is so important!! Thanks for sharing! Some of the others were still doing the dance of the Donta! Donta!! They adore how it keeps away bad energy and only brings happy, good things!

Maximus asks them to get on point. Be ready for anything to happen! Always have your guard up. It is super solid stuff!! Chase radioed over to Mider; We are having a great time. Amazing job you two are doing! Mider says you bet! Thank you! Miles said you both are very smooth at driving the boat! I'm impressed! Both said thanks; we have been taking her out in the bay practicing when you guys have been swimming at the beach! Chase and Hope smiled as did all a burst of laughter poured out of the boats!

Chase put the binos up to his eyes and magnified them to the maximum. "I can barely see our home—it's the size of an ant!" he exclaimed. "We must be only minutes away from our destination. Let's slow it down." He aimed the binoculars at their target, about a mile ahead.

"Alright, everyone, get ready! And be prepared for anything—we don't know what we might find here!"

Just then, Hope felt a strange tingling, signaling her new talent kicking in. She closed her eyes and saw, clear as day, a beautiful white bunny rabbit.

She was slumped over in a corner, shivering! Her big, long ears were dragging on the floor! Back turned, Then Hope noticed there were jail bars around and a big chain attached to the bunny's back leg! The bunny then turned and looked right at Hope! She has the loveliest big eyes! And her pupils are in the shape of red hearts!! And very long eyelashes, and started giving Hope the biggest pouty eyes anyone has ever seen!! She said hi, my sweetheart. I'm a friend; my name is Hope. What's your name? The bunny said my name is Allie! How can we see each other and talk? Hope said it's my second time, So it's new to me, too!! Hope asks are you on that big island about a half hour from that even larger Kozoway Island. Allie says I think so!? Does it have a huge statue of Atlas on the south white sand beach? Hope said yes, that's the one!

There are a few men and women that took me from my family and friends. From my small island not far west of your home. They spied on your home for a few minutes, and had me chained up and tied down! But I got to see it; it was about three in the morning. Pitch black. The moon was just a small fingernail clipping a few days ago. They backed the boat onto the beach. They had a big man-made-looking thing on the back! It looks like a metal dinosaur! One man took a draw bridge-looking thing off the boat. Another man got inside the monster, and it made a rumbling noise!

And it moved off the boat and ripped through the sand! Up to your atlas statue, the other man who was walking with it stopped at the same time. Got a chain out of this scoop-looking thing; Hope said I bet it's a bobcat!. Allie said like the animal? Hope said no and smiled. It's a man-maid thing! O wow! Said, Allie! Sure, it is remarkable. Humans can make such stuff! Isn't it, though replied Hope! I am not one of those people. I am blessed with a few talents, but that's not one of them. We all have our talents, though, Allie said! Isn't that the truth!? Both of them are saying that at the same time! Both burst out in laughter!! Classic, said Hope. No two ways about that said, Allie. Having that lovely bonding moment and loving duel smiles was such a boost of morale for both of them, bringing them closer. Looking at the situation was such a perfect bonus! Hope said, do you notice my face getting bigger, closer, my voice stronger, clearer? Because you sure are, Allie! Absolutely said Allie, then both saying we must be very close to each other. Then that is so cool! Both burst out in their fun, bubbly cackle giggles!!

Hope says. I know it's not the best time for smiles, but on second thought, smiling always does help! Here here! Said Allie. The bunny continued her story, so the scoop went through the sand, and your great breathtaking stone statue fell into it! Those dirty, rotten pieces of garbage!! Gosh, Dagg thiefs! I understand a squirrel taking a peanut and things of that nature… but the nerve of them coming to my home and being the most low-down type of thief! Next to taking from children, elderly people, animals, churches!! Allie agreed and then said they took it to the boat, put it on, and then put the draw bridge away. Then they took me here where you and myself are, caged me!! Hope said all is okay now! Keep your chin up always!!! Allie said thank you! I will! You will get rescued. I can tell you are good like myself! The good side, the light side, always prevails over the evil darkness. Hope said just as I was saying, look, God's rainbow is coming down over you, Allie! Allie just then looked up! That same rainbow that came to Hope and their family quickly shone down on her cute little bunny face!

Allie says this is a great sign…. A sign from the big guy!! The God of Gods himself!!! Allie was hit with the most incredible, one-of-a-kind, pure rushes of love!! Top shelf levels of euphoria!! Then her long ears stood straight up, and all the hairs on her pretty white fur coat puffed up!! Then she started hopping up and down!! A golden chain and pendent slid down the lord's rainbow and then went around her neck! Oh my goodness! You could not have said that better, Hope. Allie then had a 100 percent focus on Hope's chain and pendant. It's the same one you have, Hope. She nodded yes. It's now the ultimate way to test out my theory. That you are one of the good guys and gals!?

Just then, Allies red heart pupils grew larger and larger! A single tear formed out of an eye and ever so slowly ran down her bright white fur. A single pure as pure gets… joy!!!

"Well, there we go," Hope said with a warm smile. "If you were dark and evil, that tear would have turned black and turned to ash. Welcome! I'm Hope Kozoway, and this is my loving husband, Chase. Our family has just become whole."

Allie's voice was full of gratitude as she replied, "I'm deeply honored."

Hope beamed. "We're coming for you soon, sweetheart. And now that you're a Kozoway, with our new blessed powers, you have the strength to break that pathetic chain on your paw—if you truly need to."

Allie tugged on the chain until it was taut, and with a surge of energy, a link cracked in three places. "Incredible!" she gasped.

"Now, put your faith in me," said Hope gently. "Wait until we get there to free you, but remember—you have the power if you absolutely need it."

Allie nodded, her heart swelling with trust. "I fully trust you, my sister, Hope."

# Chapter: 5

And to finish my story, I did get to witness them put your statue in the backyard courtyard beside their mansion. I'm down in the basement, slash torture chamber, slash wine room. This place pales in comparison to Kozoway Island, not even half the size. Just then, both Allie and Hope heard the sounds of keys rattling and footsteps of big boots coming closer and closer!!, Both went dead quiet… it was the main guard put in charge of Allie. He was doing his rounds to make sure she was in her cage chain and was secure. Passing code. He came up to the window on the door she is in and peered in through the iron bars… it's a very evil-looking man with creepy dark badging eyes and short black hair. He spat through the bars, and it landed… spattered all over the cold brown bricks on the floor. He then took a sip of Whiskey from his silver flask,

Down the hatch. Then, letting loose a big burp!!! And in a drunken, raspy voice, said, hey ya good for nothing rabbit thing!! Checking up on you!! Allie then lightly glanced down at her chain and pendent… worried that he would see it! It seems as though the big guy, God. Built-in a defense mechanism… only those who wore them or were good enough to see them, Got to see them!! He then yelled at Allie my name is Medaling Medaliss!! And don't you forget it!!, Allie remained quiet. He did not know that she was very intelligent and could speak fluent English, nor that Hope was nearby… watching…nor that her chain was broken… she could easily get out of her cage, cell, Past him. Medaling Medaliss spat on the floor again and guzzled back the beer in his hand, Crushed the can, and then threw it at Allie… she quickly ducked!! The can nearly missed her head, crunching into the brick, cement wall!! He lets out yet another huge belch!! Then said, I'm in charge of you!! No escape ever!!

He then walked down the hallway, yelling at yet another captive creature!! They had captured. Hope whispered holy. What a world-class piece of trash jerk he is! Allie whispered, yes, we must teach him a lesson! Hope smiled and said you bet your boots and your bottom dollar! Hahaha! Giggling at the same time! The two are definitely in sink!! And on the same side, Hope, I'm going to go back to Chase and the rest of our family for a short while to get our bearings. The game plan is to get you, our atlas statue, and whatever else needs to be dealt with around here!!

Allie, you bet, Soul sister!! Hear or see you soon. I love you and trust you! The same goes for you, Allie! God bless! And to you, Hope! She then zoned back into her body. Her presence on the ship was obvious. Chase said your back. Gave her a huge hug! They then shared a lover's passionate kiss. Glad to be back, Chase. Yes, the energy around you changes, Feels hollow! Your pretty eyes go distant. And if we say something to you. There is no response. Hope said I will work on that! She then quickly told the others about her encounter with the newest family member, Allie!

Chase and the other boat had both Anchored down. The mark, The target island is a fair size still pitch black outside. They were only a few minutes away… Miles, Chase and the rest were very happy to have a new family member! Even Soul the Crow, Skye the bald eagle, and Scoops the Hawk came down from souring way up in the dark night sky! Landing on Chase and Hopes' shoulders for the new news! And the sea lovers, Lola, the turtle, and Thorn, the giant squid, were right beside the boat under an open window.

Lola is saying God bless our sister Allie! Many schools of different fish danced, And super shimmered from the moonlight! Going in circles, figure eight, Other patterns around both the boats!! Hope said isn't that breathtaking!! Miles, Chase, and the rest smiled; Miles then said okay, all we are going to take up the anchors. Use paddles for the rest of the way. I'm going to radio Maximus, Maximus… Maximus come in Maximus! Do you copy me? The two radios had both been tuned into Chase and Hope's Lucky number seven. One of their Lucky numbers, anyway.

Just as he was about to radio again, a deep voice came through— the giant lion's. "That's a big ten-four! Copy that, loud and clear. Go ahead, Brother Miles!"

Miles grinned. "Oh, I'm glad we left you in charge of home! You've always been the perfect example of the Kozoway code… strength, honor, and loyalty!"

The lion chuckled warmly. "Why, thank you, Brother Miles. You mean the world to me, too! Everything is safe and sound here. How's the quest going?"

Happy to hear that! I remember you were set on staying—you're always the one we can count on around here on the Island! And we've always called you the king of the jungle!"

He began purring and rubbed his face against the microphone, making everyone laugh. Miles grinned and said, "He's quite the character, to say the least!"

Then, Miles turned to Maximus, "Would you mind heading over to the guest mansion on the south beach? I need you to check if my best friend since we were in diapers, Heath, is there."

Chase chimed in, "He actually used his satellite phone to call mine the other day. Said he was coming off a long solo sailing trip and asked if he could stop in and stay. I told him, 'Always, brother!'"

He always did fancy that sunny South Beach side sipping on his favorite Coca-Cola classic and feasting on some of the many gourmet foods of Kozoway Island! Then Maximus said yes, I know he is a super solid man… he always has jokes to put a smile on one's face! He also has his own very amazing tasty treats!! He likes to share, Last time, we shared that smoked Hawaiian fish! My mouth is watering just thinking about it!! Yum!! The giant cat is licking his chops!! Indeed, I do say Miles, Chase also agreed and then licked his lips! Always memories of five-star stuff!! So tasty!!

Okay, I would like you and Lushis, the tiger to go over there by land and Loyal the Raven by air, also rip the great white shark by sea. Please go see if he is there… get back to us… as soon as possible! A.s.a.p.!! That's a big ten-four Miles!! I will round up those rascals and get on that! Let you know a.s.a.p. Miles replied ten- four! Miles said I Hope so we could all use his company. He is also very blessed with a talented skill set and gets an ab workout from chuckling so much!! You see, Miles, Heath, and Chase had done more than their fair share of special ops missions… standing up for the good people and such… they have a strong bond. Miles went on air again. Maximus also set up lookouts on the beaches, And when you're done, you and Lushis go set up in the lighthouse with the radio set on channel seven, please. Miles then said to turn the lighthouse on once if you guys need backup and twice if all is clear. I can do the same from both the boats and the chopper. Okay, check that, my fellow cherished fur friend! Chat with you guys soon, over and out for now. Miles then said to all the crew, please make sure both boats and choppers lights are off. And everyone, please grab an oar. There were plenty of oars on the vessels.

Useful tools to have around… come in handy. Miles then asked the beautiful birds of a feather, Soul, Scoops, and Skye, To go back to their post in the sky. Soul caaaaawwwed! Then said, yes, my pleasure! The three flew out the window. Well, everyone said, Miles, sometimes you must stand up for yourselves! Fight for what you believe in… a battle of good against evil!! For the greater good!! All the crew agreed!! Just then, all of their pendant necklaces started to glow; the gold grew bright!! The diamonds flickered just like the most eye-catching, brightest stars from the heavens above!!

Chase said, Oh no! We just made sure all the lights were off! Hope said not to worry, my king. Allie put that to the test with that dirtbag guard that is watching her! Only we can see them, or those good enough to see them. All breathed a sigh of relief. All took a few seconds to admire what God is doing to their Jewelry!! Miles spoke up, okay, everyone, let's start rowing. We have Allie to help, and I'm sure others! They began to paddle…. A loud noise of bubbles brewed up from the sea! Then a snicker-cackle laugh was heard from beside the boat!!, It is a Thorn, the giant squid!! Thorn then whispered to Lola the turtle, those oars are a joke. When I'm around, one of his enormous arms came out of the sea; he said to Lola, do you trust me? With zero hesitation, she said yes with all my heart!! Lola then looked deep into Thorn's eyes.

Then both of them glanced at their glowing Jewels… his arm came over to her, then gently picked her up… all sharing a truly comfortable silence… he then put her on top of his head. They swam silently ahead of the two boats. Both boats are seventy-five feet each. He is much larger than that… truly living up to his name, Giant!! Then two of his many, many arms with suction cups, with hooks inside of them, shot out fast out of the water!! Both at the same time are wrapping around the gold and brass railings of the two boats… quickly! Deadly quickly. Picked up speed. All crew members see the paddles are useless at this time!! Miles said, Thank you, Thorn. No problem replied the giant!! All of them now had more time to keep an eye on this mysterious island. Chase then took out Hope's pair of night binos, giving them to her.

They both put their binos up to their peepers. Let's spy on these creepers with our peepers! Said Chase, hahahahaaa! Chase whispered okay, slowly scan this place and see what you can see, pretty lady. Hope, You bet, my love. Boats are now about a two-minute swim from the target at this speed. Waves ever so slowly splashing over the fronts of the boats, Thorn is going the perfect speed to match the sound of the small waves they are in. and still by the cover of the night… they are shadows in the dark!! Miles said to Thorn from the tip of the boat, okay, stop in fifty feet. I can see the light coming through the tree canopy close to the center. Just then, a few others piped up. Oh yes, we can see it too!

"Okay, perfect," said Miles. "I bet it's their main compound home!"

Hope chimed in, "When we stop, I'll get in touch with our pal, Soul the crow. I'll have the three of them soar over this place to get a bird's-eye view."

Suddenly, the radio crackled to life. "It's Maximus. Come in, Miles. Do you copy? Over."

Miles grabbed the receiver. "Yes, ten-four. What do you have for me? Over."

"Well," Maximus began, "Lushis and I just reached the tallest peak, about a minute's run from the compound. We've got a clear view of the area. Heath's sailboat is anchored about a hundred feet from shore. His matching camouflage-painted Zodiac is tied down on the beach with a rope and a wooden stake in the sand."

Maximus paused, then added excitedly, "The wind just shifted— I can smell one of Heath's famous barbecues! Oh, this is divine!"

"Seconded!" Lushis chimed in, putting a paw up to his salivating chops and licking it a few times. "I have to try some of that delicious-smelling food!"

"You know it," said Maximus with a chuckle. "You're in for a real treat! This barbecue smells just as good as Chase's legendary grilling skills!"

Both are red seal chef trained. And their own natural original recipes!! Secret scrumptiousness!! I agree, said Miles. Hope then giggled with delight, "Me, too," said Hope! Chase smiled, and Maximus said I can smell Alberta steaks. They are the best in the world!! And lobster and Crabs from Nova Scotia are just the best!! Also, his lovely stuffed bacon and cheese mushroom caps!! O boy! O boy!! Okay, my troops, keep your wits about you. Use your gut instincts; we are on a quest. Scamper down there and see if he needs a hand with anything, and get that grub in you!! Get Heath to radio me, then go to the lighthouse as planned. Check that said Maximus. All our lookouts on the beaches and other spots have said negative on any activity; all clear here! Ten-four, said Miles, over and out for now. Ten four said the cat, over and out. Soul soured down, the sound of his talon claws connecting with the ship's golden rail was about… he let out three caws!!! All looked over at him. He let out a

Raspy, frog-in-throat cackle laugh… cakaaaa cakaakaaa cakaakaaaa. He then said I can see a man-made light about the middle of the island and some men and dogs walking about. Miles was sitting right beside him, said well done, my feathered friend!! I just saw that light, too! You see our powers!! United as a team of good, we are unstoppable!! God willing!!! All their Jewels danced! Sparkling!!!

# Chapter: 6

Just after that being said. Miles then pushed play on the CD player and turned the volume way down. One of his favorites, Frank Sinatra's song 'I Got You Under My Skin,' came on; they all had a little dance… Groosefraba, the polar bear, said, I can feel some very negative vibes coming from this place. I can also see an extra black liquid haze over it!! Soul said yes, this place gives me the creeps, too!! The crow then spoke of how he loves how we all can still caaa, growl, howl…. And speak to each other! It's a no-kidding-around advantage! In so many ways!!! Here, here said Miles!!! Lola, the turtle, spoke up. She was swimming around and then went back on top of Thorn's head… the other turtles, fish, and sea creatures won't go near this place!!! Soul said, nor will the other feathered fellows!! Not one!!! It's not surprising at all, said Hope, bad vibes… I've seen firsthand what they have done to our beloved Allie!! A prisoner!! Not for long, though!! The radio came a series of furious crunching and munching noises, then some chewing, gnawing, lip-smacking!! Maximus, with a mouthful of treats, started speaking. Chops are full of food… Miles… O boy!! Are you guys missing out? Lushis was so in awe… he could not even talk!! That's one of the true signs of a brilliant master chef!! Lushis is speechless!! Here's Heath, as you asked… Heath then took the mic from Maximus. Hello brother! How are you!? What is new? Chase came on; it's a short version for now; I'm reborn, could not be any better, very busy, on a top-secret mission, well, a quest to be more precise!! And yourself, Heath!?

How are you? What's new? … Was just about to get a hold of you or Hope… or go up to the castle… see if you two are around… is that old blue eyes I hear? Sure is… hahahaaahaaaa! Classic!! You bet!! Yes, myself as well couldn't be any better.

Came off a long sailing trip with our best Buddy, Tuffy!! Tuffy is a giant, fluffy, white, handsome German Shepard-husky. Very sharp, Heath's loyal sidekick. Tuffy then let out a bark and then a huge howl!! His two other best Buddies came over Miles, hey, Tuffy!! Then Mider, Chase's Jack Russel Terroir, woke up out of a slumber… he was having in the captain's quarters; he let out a quiet bark and howled, jumped ships, came over to the mic to say hi!! This time, Mider spoke English to Tuffy… Tuffy spoke back!! Mider asked do you and Heath have new gold and diamonds around your necks!? Heath burst out!! Hey! What's going on here!? Tuffy and I had these mysterious yet lovely Jewels come to us down a rainbow!! Miles then put Sinatra's song 'I Got the World on a string; Frank can sum up how we are feeling!!' Top of the World! Love, bliss, joy!!!

Welcome to the club, Heath and Tuffy, Miles said with a huge grin on his face!! All of us have them, God's creatures of Kozoway Island as well, air, land, sea… we have the same Jewels! Top shelf levels of cool!!! So super!!! Miles, I'm sure you get the gist of it… Heath. That's a big ten-four!!! The cats have filled us in and do what needs to be done on that strange island near us. We will help around here unless you need us… no, we love you there, for now, big Buddy said Miles… okay, little Buddy! Please help out around there. Keep a radio with you ten four said, Heath. We are going down to the beach now and see what we can see… over and out for now. Miles said okay, our triples, Soul, Scoops, Skye, please go check things out. Thorn and Lola, also go see what you can see. Miles said, " Thank you, Thorn, super stealth ride you give. He said welcome before you go. Could you please tow us ten feet from hitting the bottom?

There was enough room for the propellers to turn over and start up. Miles turned to the crew. "Mider, Groosefraba, once Thorn has us in position, please anchor both boats. We'll wait here for all of you to return and report back with what you see."

Before anyone could respond, Thorn quickly maneuvered the boats near the beach. Then, like a flash, he sped off with Lola, the graceful turtle, close behind. Mider, ever the agile one, jumped between the boats with ease. In a single fluid motion, he snatched a strip of self-hunted, smoked mallard duck jerky—one of his favorite treats—and timed his steps perfectly to fall in sync with Groosefraba out on the decks.

The swift bear caught sight of Mider's antics. Locking eyes with the dog, he watched as Mider, with a smirk and impeccable aim, tossed a strip of duck jerky straight into the bear's waiting jaws. The polar king caught it effortlessly with his gleaming pearly whites, savoring the treat. Both animals devoured their respective snacks in an unspoken show of camaraderie.

The bear gave Mider a respectful nod, and Mider returned it in kind. Then, as instructed, they dropped the anchors simultaneously. On their way back to their spots, they exchanged brotherly grins, their shared respect evident in their smiles.

"Well, I guess we'll hang tight and keep watch with the night binoculars," said the alpha wolf, Miles, his sharp eyes scanning the horizon. "Hold down the fort." Then, glancing at his sister, he added, "Except for you, Hope. I sense something…"

Hope smiled, her confidence unwavering. "Yes, Miles, your instincts are flawless as always. I was just about to check on Allie for a minute."

Miles nodded but didn't reply.

Chase stepped forward. "Okay," he said softly. "I love you."

"As do I, Chase," Hope replied, her voice tender. They shared a loving, heartfelt kiss before Hope turned to leave.

"Goodbye," Chase whispered.

"Goodbye," Hope replied, her voice lingering like a promise.Just then, the door to the bottom level of the boat opened… it was part of the good, yet extra badass part of the team. Kozoway, Ozzy!!The Kodiak bear, The head of security, With the rest of his sidekicks, Wrecker the wolverine, Wisdom the red fox, umbra the racoon and Whiskey the weasel!! A huge cloud of cigar smoke came up, and Wisdom was standing there with a cigar burning in his mouth; he had a puff off of it, Smiled, and then did a shot of Whiskey. The rest of them were sitting around the poker table, playing poker, smoking cigars, and drinking Whiskey. Wisdom asked are we sitting beside the island... watching it? You are so sharp Miles said. Yes, we are! Wisdom asked if they needed help. Miles said, yes, we need a land crew to go in and have a gander, a good look at the compound and some of this island. Stick together, be extra sneaky, stealthy! No worries said, Ozzy. Okay, gents, said Ozzy, let's go fold down your cards, continue later... finish up those Whiskey shots and put out those stogies!!

They all came up to the top deck and then jumped over into the shallow sandy waters. Miles said hey, pals, please take this radio with you. Please report back what you see. They said no problem. Miles tossed down the radio and a couple pairs of night binos, Ozzy catching them in one of his enormous paws!! Okay, talk soon... later, troops!! They all disappeared into the cover of the night jungle. Hope was already watching over Allie and her situation... still being the same, hanging tight, being smart by laying low. Hope said to her great job! Such temptation, I'm sure!? Very mature of you, Allie. Thank you she said. I figured what you said makes the most sense! The best chance of getting out of here is to unite with my new family members!! Perfectly put said Hope!

I have a very positive feeling my new blessed powers have something much faster in store to get you out of there, Allie! Oh yeah, said the white bunny, you look extra focused! You have a ladybug coming out of your front pocket!! Hope looks down, O cool!! This is Lucky. Apparently, you're a very deep sleeper, old pal!? Lucky crawled out of her front pocket and then onto her shoulder. And super sleepy-eyed. Looks into Hopes's eyes, letting loose a slow yawn. Lucky spoke up and said such a perfect slumber! Best nap ever!!! The dance of the donta donta! Champagne with a furious feast!! Went into your pocket for a siesta nap.

# Chapter: 7

Hope says it looks like you have a gift to travel with me when I use my new powers!! Hahaha!! How lovely, Lucky!! I've, we have been in this realm with Allie. Our bodies are a few minutes from here, back on one of our boats! I can leave my body. The first time I did it was at the feast. I was at the beach and then ended up chatting with Stampers, the big-eared beast in the castle living room. Then moved him to the beach feast!! In this same situation. Talking together in this dream-like state, then a little bright white star appeared!! It feels like another one is very close to the three of us is in stored! Getting those same tiny butterflies in my tummy. Lucky, I think you came out of that pocket at the same time God blessed Allie at getting out of that jail cell… that evil place!! Lucky said this is something else!! I feel like I'm dreaming still!! Hope said I know that sparkly white star is near, again… then…. Pop!!! It just popped!!, Up!!! Okay, Allie, there we go!

Both Allie and Lucky exclaimed at the same time, "Yes, Hope! Feels like in about three seconds, you'll be on the boat with us!"

The ladybug, blessed with extraordinary luck, chimed in, "I say we've got extra luck on our side!"

At that moment, all three of their jewels began to glow brightly. Then—pop!—the trio suddenly appeared on the boat.

Hope blinked as she regained awareness in her body. Lucky remained perched on her shoulder, glowing with excitement. A second later, Allie materialized out of thin air.

Reacting quickly, Hope stretched out her arms and caught the small, fluffy white bunny mid-air. She pulled Allie close to her chest, holding her tightly in a warm, affectionate hug.

Then said, everyone, this is Allie!!! Allie then locked eyes with Miles. Both of their ears perked up, as did their posture!!, Holding the deep eye lock in an intense passion!!! Miles ran over to them, and Allie ever so gracefully hopped out of Hope's arms onto the king of the handsome alpha wolves! She then gave him rapid, fast, small love kisses all over his face!! He repaid the favor by licking her cheek and then sharing a hug with her! Miles said, Allison!!, I was wondering about you!?, Everyone was saying Allie… should have put more thought into that!!, Put it together… I have to say I adore Allie… Allie care bear!!, It's suiting and very adorable, Just like you!! She instantly turned beet red, blushing all over her little bunny face!! Beet Red cheeks!! She said, "Aw!!! Thanks, honey!! It makes me blush!!" All beside them were in total awe… speechless!!! Miles spoke up. This is my best friend and lover!!

Everyone's jaws dropped even more!! Miles then said, show them; then we can have a proper kiss and hug, my love… you see, Allie has been hiding a secret, part of why she was hunted, captured, and held captive in this evil island's prison. Okay, my handsome man!!, Then, right there, in front of everyone's eyes, she transformed into a giant white fluffy wolf, just like Miles!!! Besides Miles and Allie, all's eyes grew as large as saucers!!! They both locked into a long, super passionate kiss. She is about twenty-five pounds lighter than Miles. Also, having those strikingly super pretty eyes. she was as lady-like as he was handsome. Both have the same red-hearted shaped pupils!!, Shooting hearts back and forth to one another!! Chase said this is her, hey!! Miles had spoken of her at a beach feast back home.

Chase said to Allie you have the power to change into a bunny or a wolf!? That's amazing!!!. Can you do anything else!? Not that I'm aware of, she said. The shape-shifting runs in the family, though. Very cool replied Chase. Incredible! So this is the famous Allison you spoke of, Miles. You bet, he said. Then, a couple of couch potatoes awoke. Both have a big yawn and stretch! It's Chica, the cheetah and Jewel, the snow leopard. Jewel said what a lovely nap!! Lucky laughs!! I also had a great slumber after the food, drinks, and dancing!! Hahahahaaahaaaa! Jewel then said nice to meet you, Allie, likewise. Jewel then said I overheard Ozzy and them leave on a ground mission. Chika and I are going to pitch in to help them. Besides, we cats do not even need night binos! We are good to good to go! Well, that's so kind and caring of you both said, Hope. Thank you, sweet of you to say, replied Jewel. God bless! Both cats had another stretch and a few laps out of their bowl of milk, then leaped out the window. Jewel quickly picked up the scent of Ozzy and crew, then saw the trail of pawprints in the sand, following them into the tropical Forest.

Hope asks Allie are you okay? Did they do anything to you, Harm you? No! No! Thank God!!! You saw that medaling Medaliss;

he just yelled and burped a lot, Spat. Threw beer cans. Quite the cartoon character, isn't he!! Isn't he, though … Hope is a mean son of a gun!! Bet he's capable of much more!!, Miles asks who else you know of that lives on that island? She said I'd tell you in a second. We must go there right away; there are at least a handful of captured creatures in the main compound basement. That's why we are here, said Miles, on a quest to make things right!! So, who all lives here? Besides Medaliss, there are three other men in charge; the leader is Jumpy Jack! Miles asks, Do you call him that? Allie, that's what the others call him, mainly behind his back. There are also Buck and Bob, whom I know the names of.

Also, there are a bunch of troops that are in and around the compound that take orders from Jack. And a few dogs that I noticed and heard. I listened to a few of them chat about Jack, where they kept me. Mainly the temper he has been known for. Gets so mad he jumps off things, desks, and walls, and he's extremely paranoid!! You see, he is an evil person and hunter. They are thieves who hunt and then sell what they capture and trade… they have been hunting and stalking my bloodline family and myself for quite some time. The last time was for about a week on our small island.

Jack was close to me and came up super slow and stealthy as I was enjoying a patch of Clover; I was just in wolf form minutes before. I was enjoying a white-tailed deer I had taken down and needed some greens to wash down the red meat. Impressed by his soft steps, I perked up my long bunny ears when he was ten feet away, then glanced at him before I high-tailed it out of there!! He noticed my red heart-shaped eyes. I saw the evil greed in his dark, shady eyes; he quickly dropped the shotgun he had in his hands, only to grab a slingshot from his hunting belt and loaded it! Took aim!! Then, took a shot. I turned, Glancing at him, and leaped off a bolder, the ball bearing nearly missing my head. Bet he was just trying to stun you and then capture you, said Miles. Allie nodded yes.

"He'd been tracking us for a while. I think he knew I could transform into a wolf," Hope began, her voice steady but laced with the weight of her memories. "I had to shift to save my mum. In the chaos, I injured one of Jack's troops and managed to escape to one of our last-resort hiding spots.

"I barely had a fraction of a second to act—to ensure everyone's safety. Then, behind me, I heard the chilling sound of a shotgun being cocked. I froze, not for myself, but for the greater good of our family.

"Jack's voice rang out like a death sentence: 'Buck! Bob! Get her in chains and throw her in a cage!'"

"I let them take me, figuring I'd find a way to escape sooner or later. Jack's island was crawling with guards—twenty at least, though I stopped counting after that. Jack was furious. I overheard him ranting about vengeance, claiming I'd attacked them and wrecked their operations.

"Honestly? I'm glad I did," she said with a faint smile. Then she turned to Miles. "Is it true what I've heard?"

Miles nodded grimly. "Yes. They came to our home, sticking their evil noses where they didn't belong, pretending to care about our well-being. But we knew better. We all got a strange vibe from them."

Hope's eyes lit up. "Thorn," she said softly.

"That's right," Miles confirmed. "Thorn saw to it that they never felt welcome. He scared the life out of them, made them tuck their tails between their legs, and they floored it back home."

Hope's expression darkened. "If I had known they had you— and others—or had the audacity to steal our Kozoway statue…" She trailed off, her voice trembling with emotion.

Miles finished her thought, his tone fierce. "We would've ended that battle right then and there."Anyways, moving forward!!, So they plan on attacking Kozoway Island!!! Chase, Hope. Turned beet red!!! Miles and others growled!!! Allie said yes, as far as I know… jumpy Jack had planned to go there for war with you guys and try to take over the island… hahaha… laughter all around!! That would never happen, said Miles. Good always wins over evil, replied Chase! God willing, said Miles!! Miles then radioed Heath and Maximus. Both picked up, saying go ahead, Miles… then both of them let loose their own unique cackle laughs!!, Miles spoke up, Holy!! You guys are something else!!! You are very on point, gents… and those cackle laughs are next-level funny!!, Speaking on point, Miles said… they have a plan to come to our home and then try and take it over!!! All having a snicker!!, Those dirtbags!!, It's never going to happen, Heath said. Tuffy let go a howl… yes he seconds that notion!! Maximus spoke up. Yes, Lushis and I are in the lighthouse. We cannot see anything but our beloved killer whale, Kahara, coming up and down for air in the bay. And Clover, the snowy owl, that wise old Soul, has been helping us do a lot of the security work, flying back and forth, keeping tabs on a full 360 view of the island.

She just came back from checking in with Kahara, and from A to Z, all the creatures help to keep watch; there is nothing out of the normal here… well keep up the five-star work!! Well done, replied Heath and Maximus. Meanwhile, the two cats, Jewel and Chika, were gaining fast on Ozzy and crew, Scampering very close to a well-used path… you see, cats are curious most of the time, secretive. Jewel whispered to Chika, do you hear that!?, She nodded yes, Both hearing some small scurry, ruffling of sand, leaves… both looking left the sounds about ten feet away. The noise's getting closer and yet closer!!!, Both cats stopped dead in their tracks! Not flexing a mussel!!, The scampering sounds of multiple tiny legs going through the sandy tropical forest!!, Kept continuing, nearer and nearer!!

# Chapter 8

Out popped!!! An enormous King Crab!!! Hissed!! Claws, ready!! Then both smiled at the sea barnacle!! Large for a Crab, yet pales in comparison to them!! Not a threat. The Crab saying my name is Mr. Pinches; I mean you two no harm!! Jewel hissed at him!! Both fluffed up their fur, ears back!! Dominate paws, claws out!!!. The Crab is being put on the spot!! He said I'm a friend!! Jewel, Be careful what you say!! I have nothing to hide; I'm one of the good guys like you two!! I'm one of the original Crabs and creatures that inhabit this fine red-sanded island!! Before these evil people came here and took it over, so far they have wrecked our home!!! That's no good, jumpy Jack and crew!!

Both cats retracted their claws and rested their paws back in the sand.

"I hear you; tell me more," said Jewel.

Mr. Pinches cleared his throat. "How often do you see a crab in the forest?"

The cat tilted her head, thinking. "Come to think of it, never."

"Exactly," said Mr. Pinches. "There used to be hundreds—thousands of us. Now, those who remain are either trapped, eaten, or sold."

"That's terrible!" Jewel exclaimed. "Not cool at all! But if what you're saying is true, and you're one of the good guys, we'll fix it. Don't worry. Time will tell."

"Time will tell, sooner than you think," Mr. Pinches replied cryptically.

Jewel's ears perked up. "Hmmm… that's strange, even for this place. Wait, can you see what's around Chika and me?"

Mr. Pinches nodded. "Yes, I can—gold and diamonds. It's odd you didn't mention it, but cool that you kept it to yourself. No time wasted!"

Suddenly, a small rainbow arced down from the sky, scattering jewels around the crab.

"Holy mackerel!" Mr. Pinches shouted. "What on God's green earth is going on?!" O wow!! It's the same as what you two cool cats have on!! Now I can sense you will get to keep it; I get a positive vibe from you… my name is Jewel; this is Chika. Pleased to meet you two said Mr. Pinches!! It seems as though a gift from God is here to stay for the three of us!! What do you mean, asked the Crab!? Well, if those Jewels are meant to be, they are meant to be!! They would have turned black and then fallen off by now!! Oh my, that's nice to know!! Feel more than certain that I've found myself free and clear! Found me home!! You sure have Mr. Pinches replied Chika!! You may come with us so long as you're nice and quiet!! Okay, no problem, whispered the Crab.

Just have to tell you, cats, this place is evil now, not to be taken lightly!! I'm a blessed sneaky by nature, king of crabs; I mean, who doesn't adore and love King Crab!! Don't get me started said Jewel!! Right!!! Said the Crab!! Keep your guard up even higher in this surf and turf!! Duly noted, said Jewel!! Thank you, my o so tasty brother!! Then, licking her chops!! Then winked at him!! Just kidding, Mr. Pinches, That's not funny!! Chika smiled; it was a tasteful joke, though… just jokes, Mr. Pinches!! The two cats picked up on Ozzy and crew's scents and then started to follow their paw prints again. The Crab close behind…

Ozzy then came on the radio… in a low whisper. Miles, do you copy? Miles picked up, also in a quiet whisper, go ahead, big guy… we are just outside the main compound. So far, we have seventeen guards scoped outside and also caught sight of two bosses inside through the windows; I'd say another five guards inside…with them. Okay, check that said, Miles. Okay, well, between everyone who is here, I do not think we will need any reinforcements!!? What do you think… Ozzy whispered I know in my heart of hearts we can handle this… besides, it's smart to have a bunch of us guarding home! Ten-four, said Miles; okay, you guys hold your position for now, please. Over and out for now. Check that said Ozzy. Vine, the snake, slithered halfway through the boat window; Chase looked over… he flinched slightly at the sudden sight of the slippery serpent!! O my!! Are you quiet? Faith spoke up, one of the God's Alpha Squad's members, the strong and silent type….I can't wait! Vine said to her you know it, sister!! Miles, this place is so strange!! So, I must go in for a closer look soon. I can see and hear Soul; he is souring down here as we speak.

The sound of feathers flapping. Then the crow let out three quiet caaacaaas!! He soured in through the open window and perched up on Miles's shoulder. Okay, so here is what the three of us have seen so far… one main home, all fenced off. Two guards per gate. And another fifteen, keep the outside perimeter. Then, a handful of men inside. All have guns and knives; all windows are covered with bars. Having spent a few minutes on the master bedroom balcony, this jumpy Jack and the people around him are planning on going to our Kozoway Island for revenge for what happened to them earlier. Miles said okay, thank you. It's not too surprising, I'm sure we all know and feel that they would try something… such as life!! Hence, we are always ready, But at the same time, we would much rather live in peace! On our planet! In the universe, for that matter!!! Here!! Here!! Said Hope!! Soul spoke up. Forgot to say some amazing news!! There are also four German shepherds!! Which are inside the fenced-off yard. We also saw our atlas statue; it's in the center of the yard… besides that, I caught sight of a Crab in the forest chatting with our two cats… Chase said that's odd, a Crab in the Forest! Miles, Very off-weird; my curiosity has peaked!! Mine, too, said Faith!! Mine, too, said Stampers!!

The elephant was laying down on the starboard deck; his long trunk came into the cabin and then grabbed a bunch of peanuts out of a sack, bringing them up to his mouth… started snacking on them… Crunch!! Crunch!! Crackle!! Crackle!! Munch!! Munch!! Quiet down a bite, whispered Miles. Remember, slow and stealth, some quiet wins most wars… old Buddy… You're right, said Stampers. Miles then grinned his fangs with love. Then the wolf said, okay, the first thing is to try and make pals with those German Shepard's. Or tie them up… Chase nodded yes. The radio came on Ozzy… Miles said go ahead.

Chief Well Wisdom pounced up a tree. Crawled up a Vine, then covered himself with shrubbery again… hopped up on the twenty-foot fence!! He's good!! We thought we had heard some mange mutts…a few of them. He just gave me the hand signal…. There are four of them. Ten-four said, Miles…. I just got that exact confirmation from Soul.

Ozzy's ears twitched at the faint sound of paws brushing against the sand, drawing closer… and closer. A heavy silence fell. Then, he heard it—two soft prrrrrs.

He froze. Silence again.

Out of the pitch-black forest, two sets of glowing green eyes emerged, piercing through the darkness.

Wrecker, the ever-loyal wolverine, stood firm by Ozzy's side, ready for anything.

"Wait a minute…" Ozzy rumbled, his voice low and steady. "I know those eyes."

"So do I," Wrecker replied, his sharp claws flexing instinctively. "Our kitty cats!"

Ozzy raised his night-vision binoculars and peered through them. Sure enough, it was Jewel and Chika.

Jewel stepped forward with a playful little meow. "We had the drop on both of you!"Both pounced out of the tree, landing in the sand in front of them! Thought you guys could use us. An awkward, choppy rustling sound then started coming towards them … o relax said Jewel; that's our new brother coming, Mr. Pinches, a nice, witty old Crab. Mr. Pinches then came out from under an umbrella tree… here I am, he whispered. They quickly introduced themselves!! Miles is on the mic again; please hold position and check that; remember, Ozzy loves you!!! We are over and out. All of them found spots like shadows in the shade. Where they could all have perfect views of the guards, dogs, and windows… meanwhile back at the boats… Miles whispered do you hear that!? The splashing… all went silent… Hope said. Besides, the surf splashes No. But I can sense Thorn and Lola are very near!! Exactly, Miles replied!! I know those bubbles and splashes anywhere. Me, too, said Mider!!

A bunch of water dripped down over the windows…, and the giant squid's arms were overtopped… he then said well, there is a bay stone's throw away from their home!! I could actually reach one of the master bedroom windows. I hoisted Lola up so that she could get a view… what did you see said Miles? I saw a man yelling at another man about being too nice to the prisoners… then slammed a door in his face. He then went and sat down in a chair behind a desk. Thorn then said I could easily carry a bunch of you over there and then get you guys up to a window and or over a wall…

Miles smiled and then whispered very solid stuff; thank you and Lola. So brave and loyal of you two!! Not a chore or a problem…the turtle nodded yes and smiled… hmmmm… Miles stews for a moment… Chase said I was thinking of Hope and myself putting on our scuba gear and coming through that bay… I like Thorn's plan said, Miles…. All nodded yes. Okay, Miles Hope Chase, Gods Alpha Squad and Lola, of course, will come with you into that bay, Thorn. Okay, said Thorn. Sounds like a real plan… I like it a lot!! Me too, said Hope. Faith and Miles said us, too!! Then the rest of the patient wolves nodded yes, all licking their fangs!!, with delight!!. Always craving a true hunt!! Not only are wolves loyal to their mate and squad… pack…., but they adore the thrill of the hunt, the adrenaline Heart pounding… life or death, jumping over crystal clear creeks, breathtaking babbling brooks… blood, dirt, sweat and tears… sharp strategic attacks with side dishes of fancy flanks…tricks passed down from their family trees. That always gets things done. Scrumptious tasty treats on the hunts and victory in battles… Faith said I'm nearly done waiting." Miles nodded yes. And Allie and the rest of the two boat crews.

Miles said, well, let's get this party started!! Lola does a cannonball dive off of Thorn's head!! Into the sea, the splash covered all those who were not covered behind the glass. All let out a little steam with a tiny chuckle!! Chase says very nice, Lola!! Spirts!!

Up!! Okay, I want the same crew as planned on Thorn. And go to that target spot in their bay, then I want the rest of you except you Stampers for now. Stay put, please. Groosefraba, I want you to take that sack of peanuts with you to join up with your fellow bear Buddy, Ozzy.... The big white polar bear nodded yes. Miles whispered I know how easy you can track him. You guys go join up with them. They smiled. Then, the wise intents of Groosefraba. He said let me guess, you want me to leave a trail of peanuts for Stampers to follow!?

# Chapter 9

Miles' eyes sparkled with satisfaction and delight; he had a happy grin showing with his huge white fangs, then nodded yes… Hope and Chase turned red, Blushing a bit!! Hope whispered yes, my cherished chum!! You never cease to amaze us outstandingly!! Well done!! Chase and Hope are both giving two thumbs up!! Stampers, he whispered, yes, Miles, I have a special ops mission for you…

I want you to keep our beloved cat, Perogy, with you, and have a pal with night vision. I'll radio you both if we need you to come earlier. Your extra special mission will mean the world to our family… the man who carries the world on his shoulders, our beloved statue of Atlas! It's in their backyard. I want the two of you to follow the peanut trail to the front gate. And when I say, smash down the gate! then bring it over and put it in the back of one of the boats.

Chase then whispered, "Or we could bring it over with the helicopter."

Miles liked that idea as well. Then, after a moment of deep thought, Chase added, "Hmm… come to think of it, I could use my newfound power of moving things with my mind! And with my eyes."

Hope kissed him on the cheek and whispered in his ear, "Most righteous! Solid plan so far! Miles, be safe and quiet… as long as possible! Multi-tasking more than one enemy target at a time…

nothing new that we haven't done before on other quests… for the greater good!"

Miles … I want at all costs to try our best to keep this a peaceful mission. Bring strong rope and tape to tie up any who oppose us. If need be, if your life will be lost, then use full force: Guns, knives, grenades, fangs, talons, claws… sand in their eyes…. All agree. Hope, could you please use your new gift and get in touch with all the Kozoway clan here and back home? She nodded yes. Miles, Allie, Faith, The wolves let out a quiet howl, staring up at the moon!! Chase. I want Vine to go with Groosefraba. I would think a snake of your size would make an excellent ladder for a lot of the smaller fur friends to get into the perimeter grip onto a strong tree branch that goes over their fence. Draped over, make it much quieter and simpler to slide down your slippery smoothness.

Vine said yes, well due! That's one of my specialities. His forked tongue flickered in the moonlight… Miles whispered to the polar bear; please bring a pack of that sealed beef jerky with you… it will make it so much easier to make pals with those German shepherds or lure them into a planned trap. It is going to be up to them if they are good or not!?. Mider whispered what about me, Miles!? Chase whispers it's a given man's best friend. You come with me and pals Hope, Miles… the huge, handsome white wolf. Indeed, I like you even more in the trenches, taking grenades with us. Your wits and speed come in handy!! The also very handsome Jack rustle terroir- also known as… j. Russ terortizer!! Jumped up on Miles. Licked his face, then whispered thank-you! He loved a challenge, being part of everything going on!!

Relentless, to say the least… Chase and Hope finished weaponing up and putting on their crossbows that were strapped on their wrists. Loading up arrows in them. In special pockets, grenades, smoke bombs, guns, knives of all sorts… combat, throwing… then finished putting on battle armour. Then, some war paint on their faces. And exposed skin Maximus the lion then came on the radio Miles come in… go ahead Lushis and myself just spotted a boat about a fifty footer Coming into our bay!! Near where Kahara is keeping watch, I think the killer whale instincts have taken over. Protecting the island!! Kahara is super steaming over to it!! Bee lining straight for it!!! I've never seen any whale, or anything for that matter, swim that fast!!!. I see six Souls aboard… Miles said great eyes in the sky!! The good old lighthouse! Gives all the views!! Please get a crew of creatures down to the forest edge!! Ready for anything!! Ten-four, said the cat. Keep me on this channel.

Use the radio to get others ready down there, please. Ten-four, I will also get Clover to fly down there to get a group gathered; ten-four said Maximus; let's stay on this radio channel, whispered Miles, ten-four whispered the giant cat. Also, our beloved Clover has been souring high above our island for a few minutes now… she took off so hard from the window cell… lush green leaves, blowing off nearby trees of her flight coarse… white feathers glowing in the tropic moonlight… enormous yellow eyes fixed on target, our striped pal… Lushis the tiger then radioed in… be ready. There is a boat in the bay!! Meanwhile, the extremely large whale, Kahara,… speeding- ripping towards the boat. He is an easy five feet longer and larger than their boat. Coming in super-hot twenty feet and closing… the men on top of the fine vessel, not even noticing!! The smooth and slippery white and black beast is nearly upon them!!!. ten feet… nine…eight…their captain then screamed out!! Portside!!!. Men now!!!. It was too little too late!!! Kahara's huge head lowered at full speed, then crashed into the bottom of the barge!!! Total full throttle!!! booooommmmmm!!!!!!!!! Intently putting a huge hole in it!!. Capsizing it!!! The ship then sank like a stone!!!

The noise of the crash rumbled throughout the bay and island!!!. Miles then said what that was!!… Maximus came on… Kahara sunk the enemy's ship!!!. And not one Soul has popped up to the sea's surface yet!!! O my goodness!! Whispered Miles; we heard and felt that out here!!!. What a racket!! Is Kahara okay!? Not sure. Still nothing!! Each second felt like years Or decades… then!! The big burst of an air hole…it's Kahara!!! There he is said the big cat… o phew said Miles… all breathed a side of relief. Maximus says he seems to be okay!! What a brute!! And not one of those men has come up yet!! I couldn't see anyone surviving that scene!! That wise owl Clover to the killer whale, landing on his dorsal fin. You okay, big Buddy? Kahara said I think so; Clover got a bit of a headache, that's for sure!! All of the crew is finished on that boat. The two cruised the banks of the shores for a few minutes to make sure… making sure there was no threat… Clover said one punch knockout!! Nicely done, good sir!! Thank you said Kahara. They swam over to the castle side; the big beast rested in the shallows. Clover flew off, saying I'll be back in a minute; bring you a bunch of ice for your head…. Kahara … much appreciated; see you soon.

Miles asked Maximus, "Is it all clear?"

"Check that!! Well done! Hooray!"

"Kahara, please rest up. I'm sure Clover will be back soon. Have her check the entire island perimeter, and get her to spend some extra time near the area where the ship sank."

"Lushis, I need you to come down from the lighthouse and scout the jungle for any intruders. Be sure to bring your radio with you."

Maximus, my old pal, stay solid up there as our eye in the sky. Radio Heath and keep him updated on the failed attack. Everyone, stay on high alert! That boat could have just been part of the plan… a diversion!"

"We're engaging in our quest now. We're bringing the satellite phone, but with Hope's new power, I don't think we'll need it!"

"We'll be in touch with you soon, Maximus. Okay, good luck— over and out for now. Check that," said Miles.

All were doing some finishing touches on gearing up. Chase was using his mind control talent to put camouflage paint on Hope's face and a few others. Thorn then extended one of his arms to the top of the boat, where Miles, Allie, Mider, and the rest of the wolves all slid down onto Thorn's big back. Then one of those legendary giant squid arms extended out and gripped up the larger animals, except Stampers… to prevent a bunch of extra splashing commotion…giving away their position… Miles put up his paw and saluted Groosefraba, the loyal polar bear, raised up his paw then saluted back… as did all… Lola crawled up, then set off on their course… Miles looked back, seeing the bear dropping a peanut trail behind them…all disappearing into the jungle… meanwhile, at the compound Whiskey, the weasel had just finished getting away with one of his famous talents… yet again… kind of like taking a hen or a bunch of eggs from a henhouse….

He hopped the fence and went over to one of the guard's posts. As soon as that man's back was turned, He took his sandwich and beer!! Now he thinks the other guard has taken it… the man is yelling out!! Who took my dinner!? And beer!!?? Silence …. Fine then! I guess I can't leave anything out with you guys around. One of the German Shepard gave him a stink eye… whisky, then let out a small snicker, weasel cackle laugh. Ozzy said, " I wish you would stop doing silly stunts like that!! Put us all at risk!! Blow our cover. The weasel then took a bite of the sandwich and slid down the tree, looking Ozzy deep into his eyes…. He had that ice-cold beer in his other paw. The beer dripping from the glass bottle and his tiny paw, the moister droplets hitting the sand. Pitter pater pitter pater!! On the tropic sand… Ozzy's eyes were now locked onto it. Then, in the blink of an eye, Whiskey tossed it to that giant bear!! He caught it in his paw, his razor-sharp claws wrapping around it. He licked his chops… then smiled and whispered, but you are the best at what you do!!. Like the rest of us here. He said we have not had a beer at home in a very long time…. Hmmmm, Since Heath came off his last sailing trip. He then punched a hole through the bottle cap with a claw… he nodded his head to Whiskey. Tipped it, finishing that beautiful Belgium beverage in one smooth, long sip!! A true satisfaction in his eyes… he then wiped the foam from his face with his paw. Ahh!! Thank you!! Whiskey gave him a friendly nod back… he then gave what was left of the submarine sandwich to his close pals to share, all smiling, grabbing paws fulls… Wisdom Chewing away, Says man!! This guy makes a mean sub!! All had a small snicker. Even Mr. Pinches got a piece. He looked very content!! Had not had a decent meal in a long time. There are slim pickings on this island, said Ozzy. You got that right said the Crab, munching away. My family and myself have had it so rough here. Plans of moving in the works….Soul then soured down, landing on Ozzy's shoulder and went shhhhh…. One of the dogs is nearing here.

All went silent. Soul was munching on some sandwiches, while Wisdom, perched at the top of the fence, was covered in mud, shrubs, and leaves. He gave Soul a look, as if to say, Yes, I see him too. The jingle of the choker chain grew louder, the sound of paws hitting the pavement, and the panting of a long tongue grew nearer… closer…

The wind was in their favor. Earlier, when Whiskey had been in the yard, he'd sprinkled black pepper around them—an ingenious tactic he'd seen Chase use. One whiff of that pepper, and the dog would lose his sense of smell for weeks. He wouldn't be able to sniff them out.

It was a beautiful thing.

Everyone was still as statues. Stealthy quiet, some even holding their breath. The dog sniffed the air, his ears swiveling like satellite dishes, eyes wide and unblinking, intensely focused. He scanned every angle, searching for hiding spots. His gaze paused as he looked up at the leafy branch where the fox was camouflaged.

The dog's eyes widened. The whites of his eyes were hidden by the shade of the leaves, and a sliver of moonlight cast a pale glow over the island. Wisdom, nor the German Shepherd, moved a muscle. They locked eyes. The shepherd's breath fogged in the cool moonlit air.

The crafty fox realized the mangy mutt couldn't see him. He crept closer to the pepper patch. Just two feet away…

Then, a man came out of the house and whistled three loud times. The other three dogs immediately dashed toward him. He began tossing steaks for them. But the fourth dog, Gunner, stayed where he was, staring at the leaves.

The man, now spotting Gunner with his flashlight, shouted, "Gunner! Get over here! Now!"

Gunner broke his focus for a moment, turning his right ear toward the man. He held his stare for a few more seconds, sniffed the air, and then sprinted toward the steaks

.

# Chapter 10

The sounds of Gunner's collar, paws, and pants of his drool-filled tongue dissipated. They could still hear the man yelling. Gunner barked; he got thrown a steak!! What did you see over there, boy!? Gunner is just staring at him, chopping on his supper. The other three dogs finished their supper and started walking towards Gunner, wanting more to eat… he then let out a fierce growl!! Snared flashing his fangs, ears back, the hair stood up from his neck down his spin, tail puffed up too!!! He's staring them all down. The three back down, walking away in different directions to keep watch on the property's perimeter. Ozzy said well! You sure put that hiding spot to the max and it passed the test!! Wisdom glanced at him with love and great confidence, winked at him, then flicked his long and bushy red and white tail around his chest!! Then, asked Ozzy if he had the rest of that beef jerky. The bear nodded yes, then said of course!! Perfect, says Whiskey, indeed replies Wisdom. It's going to be too easy to trick those mangy mutts!! All have a chuckle.

Meanwhile, Thorn's ferry ride, all still aboard him, is going smoothly; Mider had to be right at the front ahead of everyone. Nose pointed up, sniffing, snorting, and sneezing into the sea air! Classic dog style. Hope said look at him! All glanced, then snickers. Just like when we take him for a car ride, sticking his head out the window… doing that!! Miles, doing the same thing as Mider, burst out laughing. Then both have another good sniff! Mider looked over at Miles, smiled, and then sneezed!! Miles, Bless you. Mider, wiping his nose with his paw, said thank you. Thorn said, "Oh, I nearly forgot. Chase says what's that? There are bars I'm going to lift you up to. I can tear through them like a hot knife through butter. Then I'll put them down at the bottom of the bay. Perfect, said Miles. No problem replied the squid. Hope, I can feel this place very well now; no surprise it is super evil! The men who run it anyway. I can see seven prisoners in the basement, where they kept Allie. Allie said that sounds about right! Hope they are all fur friends- pals. No humans. All scared and afraid, not for long!! Said Faith!! God's Alpha Squad is ready to rip this place up to shreds!! Thorn, we are a few minutes away from our target. Chase said perfect!! Hope asks if I could check in with Heath and Maximus to see what is going on. Chase smiles; exactly, my love!! I see you are on it! Very on point!! I brought the satellite cell phone just in case. But wow!! Thanks, you're so cool!! Hope blushed, then went into her mode… focusing, thinking of Heath and Maximus… she could see inside the beach house.

Heath and Tuffy are both sitting on the couch finishing off their barbeque feast supper. They have the whole wall of televisions, going Chase, Hope, Miles, Heath, Tuffy and Mider all love movies, nature shows, and sports… from time to time. Heath a little more so. O classic Heath, she had a view from behind them. Tuffy barked. His friendly bark, though. They both know her voice… both turn around to see her, thinking she's right there… behind them in the flesh. Both of them are now looking all around the room. Thinking they are getting a prank pulled on them. Hope is staring down from up near the living room ceiling. She asks if anything is good? Heath's eyes light up. He can see her now!! Tuffy lets out another howl. Looking all around? No, no, said Heath up there, Tuffy! He points at her. Tuffy looks, then locks eyes with her, whines a little bit, and starts to wag his tail. Hi Tuffy, I miss you too, good Buddy!! She then extended her arm down, shaking hands with Heath, then gave Tuffy a petting on his head.

"What the?!" Heath exclaimed. "I know—it's new to me too!"

"Is everything okay?"

"As far as I know, I was waiting for a reply from Maximus," Heath said. "We were just about to head down to the sailboat to see if we need to come to you. Where are you?!"

"I'm here," came the reply. "And my new powers… let me do this!"

"Very cool," said Tuffy. "Lots of new powers all around, to say the least!"

"Hope… just stay here for now, please," Heath continued. "We just reached the target. I can sense it's only loved ones and peace on our beloved Kozoway Island. Stay in touch with Maximus, well due."

Before he could finish, Hope vanished into thin air.

"That was unreal!" Heath said to Tuffy.

"Yip," the dog barked, grabbing a turkey drumstick from Heath's hand and beginning to munch on it.

Heath smiled. "I love you, little buddy."

Tuffy wagged his tail. "I love you too, big buddy."

Heath placed the radio back on his lap, leaned back, and started to enjoy the view.

Meanwhile, Miles and his team were nearing the compound, entering the bay.

"Okay, Thorn, can you lift us up to that top window? It's about forty feet up."

"No worries," said the giant squid. "My reach is longer than that."

"Amazing," Miles said with a grin.

"Alright, everyone," Miles instructed. "Once we're inside, stay close, stay stealthy. Unless all havoc breaks loose, then… well, silence is no longer an option."

Thorn swam closer and closer, silent as ever. The tropical sun was just starting to rise, its beams breaking through the palm trees on the other side of the island.

"This is the perfect time for our introduction," said Chase. "There's a good chance people are still in their beds, or at least off guard."

The only sound was the occasional splish-splash against Thorn, who matched the natural rhythm of the sea. The guard watching their area would be gone for five minutes—first mistake already. No permanent presence at the seaside post—another crack in their armor.

The team felt a surge of confidence. Mider and Miles' tails wagged, and the wolves joined in. Miles and Faith licked their chops in sync.

Soul, perched on Miles' shoulder, flew towards the target window to take a sneaky peek. Hope focused on the window and the master bedroom.

"I see an empty bed," Hope reported. "No one in the room right now. There are two guards outside, though. One's playing video games on his phone, and the other is asleep."

"Okay, my love," Chase whispered, "Thank you. Outstandingly helpful!"

"More cracks in their armor," said Miles, nodding in appreciation of Hope's talents.

"Alright, Thorn, let's go," Miles gave the go-ahead.

The giant squid reached toward the bars of the window, silently and carefully wrapping a tentacle around them. He paused for a moment to check if anyone had heard.

Chase gave the all-clear, and Thorn softly placed the bars in the water, where they sank like a sack of hammers, almost hitting an old octopus home made of lobster traps, oak buckets, and rock formations.

A feisty octopus shot out like a rocket, releasing a cloud of ink. Thorn and the crew were momentarily surrounded by dark purple and black murk. The octopus shot to the surface to investigate.

When it saw Thorn holding up a handful of creatures, the octopus released another ink cloud.

Thorn, now annoyed, looked down. "Who dares threaten us?"

The octopus froze.

"My name's MC Maddie," the creature said. "I'm Irish. Just got here from Ireland. You almost destroyed the home I built!"

Thorn's eyes softened. "Sorry about that. I didn't know anyone was down there!"

MC Maddie chuckled. "It's alright. The men here took my family. I'm the last of us. I'm homesick, and these men are evil."

Thorn nodded. "Okay, we're pals now. If you're worthy, you'll make it back home."

MC Maddie glanced at Chase and Hope. "What about them?"

"No worries here," Chase reassured him. "We're here to make things right, to free the good souls trapped here."

MC Maddie froze, considering this. The moment stretched, and suddenly, a rainbow appeared. Hope looked at him and said without hesitation, "He's family."

Miles gave the signal, and Thorn, with precision, began to remove the window. He used one of his suction cups to pull it free and gently placed it on the sandy bottom below.

"Look at the trunk of that tree," Hope said.

Chase glanced over. "It looks like a face… eyes, nose, mouth."

"Bang on," Hope said, both staring at the tree's bark.

Then, with a whisper of magic, the face came to life. "Who goes there?" it asked.

"This is Hope, and I'm Chase," Chase said. "We're all family. We mean no harm. We come in peace, to make everything right here again."

The oak tree's voice softened. "I can tell this is a peaceful place, down to the roots."

"Well, now you're speaking my language!" the tree responded. "Thank God. You bet it is!"

"I'm Bud," the tree said, its bark creaking as it smiled. "Glad to meet you." Allie then transforms into the white fluffy bunny with red heart-shaped eyes. Bud says so it is you!! Then she turned back into a wolf; true courage coming back here!! Go get em!!! Yes, there are a few good creatures kept here against their will: a lemur, a goose. A horseshoe crab … we will not forget, and God willing, make this island and the rest of God's green earth pure!! And good again, and beyond, the galaxy!!! The universe!!!!!! Then, that friendly oak tree set his sights on making steps out of one of its branches up to the window cell for the fellow warriors. Hope said thanks, friend! He replied, "You're welcome; I thought I'd pitch in." Chase, at the top, extended his hand down to Hope; she then reached up, interlocking her fingers into his. He helps lift her up, Mider always being a gentleman, always waiting… ladies first. He then jumped up beside his loving masters, same for Miles, letting Faith go first. Thorn then joined in with his many arms, lifting up Lola, the turtle; she said I'm going to keep you company, Thorn. Besides, I'm much more handy in the water, keeping you company, he smiled. He then brought Lola close to him, ready for their next adventure. All full of butterflies in their tummies… the way it is. The Soul does truly bunch up in one's tummy when one is tested in the fate of good or bad. Every situation is unique, and life is a beautiful thing; as old blue-eyed Frank Sinatra says, the most amazing thing is love!!! Miles whispered; if all possible, the first thing is to tie up those two guards outside the door to this room. All nodded yes; Soul was perched up on Miles; the handsome wolf then whispered to him, please fly down to Ozzy and then let them know we are going in the window and to lure those four dogs. Tie them up if need be; if they are friends, bring them more of us, all the better. We will meet in the middle, the crow nodded.

# Chapter 11

Miles gave him a hug and said thanks, old brother. Soul flew off into the dawn air. Meanwhile, Groosefraba, Vine the Snake, and the company had just caught up with Ozzy and them. Vine had told them the plan as using himself as a hanging ladder from the tree… Soul flew down, landing on Ozzy, telling them they just went into the window. Meanwhile, Lucky the ladybug flew out of Hope's pocket and then went into the room they were outside of to have a gander… Hope…whispered, come back, you brave little Soul, come back!! All could hear the faint sounds of video games and snoring coming through the door; Lucky finished off her flight, landed on Hope, and then said all clear. All are giving her a loving look!! She started to blush, and then that turned into a golden glow… all their jewels shined and flickered, as did all Ozzy, Heath, and all who wore them; everyone paused and looked with deep thought to all the brave Souls on their quest…

Lucky slipped back into Hope's pocket, peeking out with one eye, ready for anything. Miles and Chase moved in cautiously, scanning the room, and then helped the others inside. The space was modest but functional, with a bathroom and a walk-in closet beside a wood-burning fireplace still ablaze. Fresh logs had been added just ten minutes earlier — a clear sign that jumpy Jack wasn't far.

Lucky whispered to Hope, "Do you want me to fly under the door and distract the two guards out there?"

Hope shook her head. "No, no, sweetheart. Don't bother. There's a deadbolt on the door."

Chase stepped forward, placing his hand on the lock. Everyone tensed, knowing that once it was opened, chaos would likely follow. He unlocked it. In an instant, they all pounced, disarming the guards with their guns and knives before gagging and tying them up faster than a cattle roping. They dragged the subdued men over to the bed, neither of them making a sound.

"Wise choice," Miles muttered, baring his huge white fangs, some still faintly pink from his last meal. He raised a paw to his lips, signaling silence. "Keep it that way. If they don't receive their jewels, we'll knock them out and stash them under the bed. Stealth is the key to victory."

Miles, Faith, Allie, Chase, and Hope all stared deeply into the men's eyes, searching for something. Miles was the first to speak. "I don't see any good in them."

"Nor do I," said Faith.

"Neither do I," added Allie.

The guards' eyes bulged as they trembled, tears streaking down their faces, yet still they made no sound. Chase turned to Hope. "Okay, my love, could you please check ahead?"

Hope smiled confidently. "Already on it, my king."

Chase grinned. "Very cool, my love." The two shared a caring kiss, then looked down at the two tied up. Miles then looked at Allie to see what I was talking about; the jewels did not even come down to them; I sure do. Then, jumping on him, also having some kissy time… Miles loving it!! Okay, okay said Chase with a giant grin. Hope is still on point, looking to what's ahead; Lucky, on that same page fly's out of her pocket and then down the spiral staircase to see what's going on. Miles then said that there was not even an attempt for them to get their jewels. He gave the go-ahead to knock them out and stash them. Hope … the next two sets of stairs are clear. Then, outside those next set of doors are two more men posted there. Both are on point in doing their job. There is also a constant flow of other guards going through that hallway. So, stepping up their game plan is here. All jokes aside, I sense those two under the bed are jokers; the rest are not. I can just see guards at the moment, one step at a time said Miles. This blessed extra sense is truly divine, staying true to them. We all love you, God!! Their jewels glowed!! Then a burst of energy flowed through their veins!! Speaking of divine, said Miles. This sensation is super next-level!!! Heaven!!! Words can't explain it; Faith and Allie… all nodded as they made their way down the stairs.

Meanwhile, with Ozzy and the crew, Ozzy has a plan for the two big leafy bushes just inside the fence. One is just beside the fence; a big branch is shooting out past the shrub. So they found a smart spot… four feet from there was a second bush. Ozzy wants to split the team up, some in one bush, some in the other, then have Vine, that slippery snake, ready for Wisdom, Whiskey, and Wrecker to slide down… a super surprise air attack!!! Ozzy had already got that wicked Wisdom to make a trail of beef jerky leading up to their spot beside the fence, where they would be waiting. Then, of course, a nice stockpile of jerky right at the front of the bush that Ozzy was in. That jerky scent will be intoxicating, in a good way… an irresistible plan. Hook, line, and sinker!! With a flank to the side and above!! Ozzy whispered okay, every one into position. He then asked Whiskey are you sure you did not put any of the jerky in the black pepper patch he left near there earlier; he nodded yes. Let's do this!! Ozzy then looked out across the yard; he spotted two out of the four mangy mutts, then he let go a loud three-set whistle… the same one he heard…. who feeds them the steaks! Then whispered get ready for anything!!

The jingle, jangle of the dog's collars began. Then, Ozzy put his claws up to his fangs and let go of that same whistle!! All the creatures are waiting above Vine, wrapped firmly around a sturdy, thick branch, ready to release into a fireman's pole. As Ozzy said, please wait for the four dogs to eat the trail, then come to the bush he's in to get more jerky. Then all the others come in from behind, above, surrounded, outmatched, and outnumbered Like a mouse trying to get the cheese in a trap But tenfold!! The hounds are on the hunt!!

The second supper whistle had them drooling. All four were united, about a hundred feet from the trap and closing in fast — now sprinting! "Will they take the bait?" Wrecker whispered.

Ozzy smiled as their paws and claws tore up the lush lawn, bringing them closer and closer. Gunner led the pack, charging ahead with the other three following in his wake. Suddenly, he skidded to a halt and fixed his gaze on the same branch that had caught his attention earlier—the one where Vine was hidden.

The others caught up to Gunner and sat down behind him, their noses twitching in the crisp, damp pre-dawn air. The wind was still in their favor, carrying the tantalizing scent of beef jerky — not just any treat, but the ultimate temptation. The smell hit Gunner first, then the others.

Gunner hesitated, his instincts making him wary. He glanced up at the branch again, then back at the first piece of jerky lying in the trail ahead. Slowly, he stepped forward, sniffing the treat before licking it. Finally, he took a cautious bite.

That was all it took. The other shepherds rushed over, noses down and tails wagging, joining in the feast. Soon, it was a full-on feeding frenzy — jerky was like catnip for dogs. They tore through the trail, one piece after another, oblivious to anything else.

One by one, they passed under Vine's perch, with Gunner — clearly the alpha — leading the pack. Just a few steps ahead of the others, he wolfed down the last pieces of jerky before reaching the stockpile by the bush.

A gust of wind blew in, shifting in favor of Ozzy and his crew. Gunner paused at the bush, sniffing intently, and began devouring the stash of beef. But as he shoved his nose deeper into the pile, his eyes widened.

Right in front of Gunner's face, two massive sets of paws and claws emerged from the shadows. He didn't need a sniff to know—he could feel it. The element of surprise was gone, and the battle was upon him.

Vine quickly unraveled, unleashing its full form. Wisdom and Whiskey slid down the slippery serpent, while Ozzy pushed aside the limbs obscuring his face. His electric eyes burned with intensity as he flashed his giant white fangs, still faintly pink from his last kill.

Gunner locked eyes with Ozzy, both of their fur bristling, bodies tense, ready for a clash. The other three shepherds turned to look behind them, only to see an entire squad staring them down. Groosefraba and the others emerged from the second bush, surrounding them.

Ozzy spoke, his voice sharp and commanding. "If I were you, I'd stay nice and quiet. Just like that." He leaned in closer, a sly grin creeping across his face. "Besides, I've got plenty more of that jerky you all seem to adore."

Gunner smiled at Ozzy… the bear then reached into the sack, taking another paw full of tasty treats out!!.. Then another!!!. And another!!! Until he emptied out the sack!!! All shared a moment in a comfortable crunching and munching… a strong bond had formed right off the hop. Ozzy then said with a mouthful of food, I think you guys will be with me. Gunner then looked up at him and said I Hope so!!.. Paused…. I can talk out loud!!! In true amazement!!! Ozzy… as I said, I have a good feeling about this!!!

Groosefraba, the polar bear, then said, we come here to make peace at this place…his two white paws came together, and then he formed a heart shape. Everyone was more at ease munching…just then, God's rainbows came down to all four dogs… Gunner's eyes light up, my name is Gunner, my name is Ozzy, we will get to names later, said the bear. Ozzys asks do you guys like it here. We noticed that man fed you all steaks. Gunner… we despise it here, Ozzy. It's a mean, lonely. Cold, the only reason we get steaks is that all of us refuse to eat dog food, the canned and kibble kinds; I mean, who would eat those!? They are disgusting!!! All had a snicker!!.. Ozzy.. You're sure right about that!!.. Shoving another piece of jerky into his mouth. Gunner.. The men make us watch. And this place is an island we have been here for so long… the jewels formed around their necks.

Wisdom, that crafty red fox, whipped his fluffy tail around his front side, then said we are about to see if you dogs are friends or foes!!? Vine slithered down the branch onto Ozzy's neck, then stuck out his forked tongue, tasting the air a few times… then, he said, this place is tainted with pain, darkness… Ozzy nodded yes, and then he said look, their jewels are still here!! You guys are family now; congrats!!! I'm glad it turned out that way.

"I have good vibes from you dogs," said Ozzy.

"Us as well," said Gunner!!..

And by the way, this is Porter, red, and taco. All nodded. Ozzy said, " I want you guys to lead as many of those guards back here… we promise to make it good around here again. Then you guys are welcome to stay here or return to our home island not far from here. All smiled, and then Gunner said no problem, most of those men are true meatheads, knuckleheads…. This will be fun!!! Jumpy Jack is the exception; he's the ring leader. Said the dog; he's pretty sharp; please don't underestimate him or the others. Okay, said Ozzy, make us proud, please!! Gunner says we will!!! Gunner… there are a lot of things to set straight around here… been here for a long time so far!!.. That jumpy Jack has made everything bad happen around here!!.. Ozzy.. We will fix it up, brother. Okay, please go. We will be here waiting. Don't worry about anyone seeing your jewels. Only good can see them. God bless, see you soon.

# Chapter 12

Meanwhile... With Miles' squad. They had made their way down the two levels of the spiral stairs and were now listening through the set of double doors. They could now hear two guards just in front and several more passing by consistently. Hope is now using her new gift. She is a fair way down the hallway. Whispers. There are a handful of guards going through here every few minutes, and I can see up the other side that there is another set of stairs leading upstairs. There are six more up there. And underneath us. In the basement, I can see the goose, a lemur, a horseshoe crab, and four more in cages. Miles… first we deal with all the men, then free those poor souls, locked up. Okay said, Chase. Then Miles whispered, Hope, when the next set of soldiers come by. Please crack the door a little bit. Then say, hey, you! Come help me!.. I bet at least a few of them come in here to see what's going on!?..

All nodded, their eyes and faces radiating confidence. They loved this flank. "Let's go with that," Miles whispered, his voice steady. "Okay, ready for anything. We'll tie them up again and leave them behind closed doors. Then, we head upstairs."

Hope closed her eyes briefly, focusing. "I see a different man," she said. "He's in a black shirt and camouflage pants, heading upstairs to the main living room. He's carrying a huge machine gun. The walls are covered with mounted animal heads. He's drinking a beer and spitting chewing tobacco on the floor… nasty fellow.

And…" her voice dropped, "down here by us, another set of soldiers will be at the door in thirty seconds."

Chase silently pulled duct tape and rope from his bag. "Get ready," Miles ordered. "Some of us will hide under the stairs; the rest will stay behind the doors."

Hope gave a quick nod. "Okay, open the doors!"

Miles opened them just enough. Hope crouched down in front of the staircase and called out, her voice trembling convincingly, "Can someone help me? Help!"

From outside, a guard groaned, "Not again."

"What do you mean, 'not again'?" another replied, confused.

"Last week," the first guard said, "one of Jack's ladies fell down the stone stairs after too much champagne. Let's check it out."

The guards crept in cautiously. Hope lay on the ground in the dimly lit room, her figure barely illuminated. One guard flicked on a flashlight and scanned the area. Three more followed behind him, the beam landing on Hope.

"Who are you? Identify yourself!" one barked.

"My name is Hope," she snapped. "Jack warned me I could get lost in this place. Now get the guns and lights out of my face!"

"Oh, sorry," the guard muttered, lowering his weapon and flashlight. He glanced around. "Did we blow a fuse again?" He pointed his light at the fuse panel. "Hey! The switch is just off."

He reached for it, but before his fingers could touch the panel, Miles, Faith, and the rest of God's Alpha Squad pounced. The team moved with precision, disarming the guards in an instant.

Chase stood back, his focus intense. With a wave of his hand, he used his mind force to slam the double doors shut, locking and holding them tight.The rest of the team then came out and tackled them, holding them down. Taping up their hands. Mouths, feet. Miles… a few of us could take them up, then put them under the bed with their pals. The rest of us will wait here, thinking up our next move. Faith said we will do it!!.. It's an honor!!.. She and a few of the wolves' then bite down on the men's clothing… shirts, belts, and pants. Lifting them up, then carrying the men upstairs.

Meanwhile, Gunner and crew's strength, honor, and loyalty seem to have stayed true!!.. Soul, that crafty crow, has just finished spying on the four dogs and other things about the gloomy island, souring down, perching up on Ozzy's shoulder, and then telling him about the dog's positive mission for them. Then mentioned there are a baker's dozen, maybe upwards of fifteen guards in the yard.

In the blink of an eye, the men on top of the main compound shone two big spotlights in and around where they were hiding!!.. They can only see the two bushes and the fence; Ozzy then says here we go into battle!!.. They then could hear the noises of the men and dogs getting much closer!!.. All had now gone back into the bushes—others up Vine, the snake in their spots. Vine then coiled up, ready for his round two to unleash his ladder talent. Now nearing full-out daylight, with the sunrise, bursts of sunbeams coming through the jungle. The men kept up their relentless use of the spotlights in and around the fenced perimeter… trying to eye up any intruders … movement… the four dogs leading the way to them barking, the crew of men with machine guns, and other weapons. Behind!!.. Mud, grass flying!! Sweat dripping!!.. Gunner is leading them now, sitting in front of the bush Ozzys in. Mr. pinches in with him at his feet. The captain and men all bunched up beside the dogs… the captain said. Are you for real, Gunner!??.. There is nothing here!!. Gunner then growled at him. A small rustling then came from the crab… all the men then took aim. Pointing their guns at the bush!!.. The captain then yelled!!.. Hold your fire!!! A few seconds passed by!!.. Then the crab emerged out of the camouflage!!.. He then yelled out again. Hold your fire!!! Then.. Gunner!!.. You made it seem like it's a huge emergency!!.. It's just a harmless crab!!.. But he will make a tasty supper for me, though!!

The crab then raised up his crusher claw, then clamping down as hard as he could on the captain's calf!.. In a true act of bravery!!.. His leg muscle sliced wide open. Gushing out blood!! He lets out a pain-filled scream!! Raised up his army boot above the crab. Just about to squish the life out of him!!.. Mr. Pinches then says. I will never be your supper!!! The captain's eyes. Light up!!.. Then, putting his foot down on the lush green grass… a talking crab!!.. Perfect!! You will be worth endless money! I will put you in a cage like the other misfits!!.. Like a lightning bolt. Skye the bald eagle.

Darted straight at his face… doing a dive bomb!!.. His razor-sharp talons, cutting into, then across his face… tearing out his eyes… then taking them with him into the jungle!!! The captain then lets out a super loud, blood-curdling, panicked scream!!! My!! Eyes!!!! My eyes!!! My eyes!!! All the men now panicked!!.. Not thinking anything through… start shooting at the Sky!! Not one of their bullets even coming close… Skye then lets loose a massive eagle scream!!.. ahhh!! Screeeeech!!!.. In victory!!!

All around, the trees, shrubs, and vines sprang to life, their leafy branches shooting out like missiles toward the guards. "This place has gone mad!" one guard yelled in panic. "This is insane!" screamed another.

In a flash, Ozzy emerged from the shadows, barreling into the nearest man with a devastating headbutt, knocking him out cold. Without missing a beat, he grabbed two more guards — one in each paw — and smashed their heads together with a sickening thud, leaving them crumpled on the ground.

The remaining guards fought desperately against the animated branches, their captain slumping over with his hands clutching his face, overcome by pain. Amid the chaos, the creatures leapt from their hiding spots. Vine unraveled, slithering down like a stealthy, slippery serpent. The group focused on disarming the guards, stripping them of their weapons and any ability to fight back.

Wisdom lunged, sinking his teeth into one man's hand, causing him to cry out in agony. Whiskey climbed up another, slithering under his shirt and digging his fangs and claws into the man's back. The guards flailed and stumbled, their cries echoing through the chaos.

The spotlights swiveled, illuminating the scene of pandemonium — branches thrashing, creatures striking, and blood staining the ground. The sergeant, eyes wide with terror, made a break for the red alarm button, desperate to activate the island's sirens. But before he could press it, the English vines covering the island erupted into action, engulfing him and the five men near him in a tangled, unyielding web.

Inside the house, Jumpy Jack pressed himself against the bay window, his face frozen in awe and disbelief. He rubbed his eyes, thinking it was a hallucination, but when he opened them, the same nightmarish scene unfolded before him.

Suddenly, the vines shifted their focus to Jack. In the blink of an eye, they had mummified the entire exterior of his home, including the helicopter perched on the roof's landing pad. The aggressive plants writhed with determination, twisting and turning the doorknob of the double French doors, trying to force their way inside.

Jack assessed the situation, his breath coming in short, panicked gasps. His eyes darted to a nearby gun rack. Without hesitation, he bolted toward it and grabbed the biggest, baddest weapon he could find.There is one in the rack. A Fully automatic AK47!!! Then his favorite, and oh so sharp, samurai sword, a few throwing knives, hatchets, and grenades!!.. He was still eying up a few more final touches on his personal arsenal.. … Crack!!! Smash!!!! The Vine have ripped more doors off their hinges!!! Then they broke their way through the bay window!!! He takes the safety off the AK47, puts the strap around his shoulder…, and then puts a fresh oversized magazine in it!!.. Then screams out. You think you can take over my island!!! Then points the gun. Aiming at the largest, fastest moving Vine heading straight at him!!.. Then starts blazing lead at the Vine!!!. It has zero problems decking out the bullets!!.. He then yells out what is going on!!! This is my turf!!! My land!!! The Vine is just plain Jain, disagreeing with him!!! It belongs to GOD and Mother Earth!!! And all the good souls of the universe!!! Jack then puts the gun in a backpack. Strapping it on his shoulders… then, like a champ, he draws out a throwing hatchet. Throws it with all his might and the best of his aim at that same Vine!! The Vine grabs it like a master ninja. Hurling at him with light speed, Jack just ducked out of the way, the Hatchett gracing his ear of the headshot then sinking into the red oak wall behind him, splinters flying everywhere!!!

He then looked down. His shoulder is also bleeding. And one of the shoulder straps sliced off, hanging down!! He groaned in pain!! Jack is gasping. Rips off his sweater sleeve, then wraps and ties it around his gushing shoulder wound, with the other arm and his teeth, pulling it tight!! He began sprinting towards a nearby room. His den. It also has more weapons inside. The Vine was close behind, trying to trip him up. Then tie him up…. Just getting inside, slamming the thick iron door shut, and locking it, the Vine the coming under the door, grabbing at him. He leaps on a rocking chair and then draws out the sword. Slicing through the arm of the chair, cutting off the very tip of the green Vine with golden sharp thorns in the process!!! The piece of the cut-off Vine turned a bright red, reattached itself, and then started crawling up the wall. Destroying a crossbow mounted on the stone wall!!.. Jack's eyes are as big as saucers!!. He turns super white, and his jaw drops!! This room only has two small stained glass windows in it with iron bars on both sides. And also a secret set of spiral stone stairs hidden under his desk. That Leeds down to the main hallway. Then basement. Jack already knows that going up the stairs to the roof is useless!! He picks up the landline phone on the desk, putting the receiver to his ear… the line is dead!!! He then goes into the side pocket of his cargo pants. Grabbing out his cellular phone. No luck with that either… zero reception!!..

The mass of vines was overwhelming, too thick for the nearest cell tower to break through. "Oh, my satellite phone!" Jack whimpered, realizing it was on his boat. "Baaahhh!"

The vines closed in, creeping around the room, working their way toward the stained glass windows. The cracking sound of shattered glass echoed through the space, followed by the deafening sound of iron bars being ripped from the stone walls.

The plants tightened their grip, surrounding him, leaving him with only a few options. In a desperate move, he drew his sword and sliced through a section of vine that had wrapped itself around the elephant tusk on his desk. With the vines closing in, Jack knew he had to act quickly—he yanked at a hidden lever, triggering the secret door.The Vine had already grown back in a New York minute. He pulls the tusk up…. The door opens!!.. The Vine now fully consumed the den… crushing the pictures, desk chairs… Jack is now sprinting down the stone steps. The vine is nipping at his heels!!! He can now faintly hear a familiar sound… the noise of his right-hand man, well, his supposed right-hand man… snoring!!! Just barely over the frantically, hectic crashing sounds around him!!! Souring splinters, paint, and stone chips flying!! He yells!!.. Medaliss!!...Medaliss!! Then, screaming, you fell asleep on your post again!!! How!!.. Dare!!.. You!!! Jack, turning bright beet red in anger, stress, pain, and disbelief at this new green and gold enemy!!..

# Chapter 13

Dripping with sweat and blood!!.. Starting to second-guess things. The thoughts of defeat are starting to sink in!!.. Fear. And then just above his lion's head, and crossbow mounted above the fireplace, on the stone, wood wall… pop!!!!! Hope appeared and said, jumpy, Jack!!! Jack jumped back many feet!!.. His eyes are frantically darting all around the room… he's now in full-out panic mode now!!.. No, no, said Hope up here!!.. You knucklehead!!.. Jack then looks up, seeing her!! With zero tolerance… no hesitation… squeezed the trigger of the AK47.!!! At that moment, Chase senses and sees Hope's path of vision. Then, he blocks the bullets from reaching her!!.. Uniting the two powers for the greater good!!..

Jack stopped, his breath heavy, his eyes welling with tears. His blood pressure was through the roof. Hope's voice echoed in his mind: "Make it easy on yourself. Surrender! You're finished! Your last guard is asleep downstairs. All your perimeter is taken care of. They're made into mincemeat."

In a desperate rush, Jack jumped up from his leather chair, which was almost entirely consumed by vines, holding him aloft above a polar bear skin rug. The vicious tendrils snapped at his feet as he quickly drew his gun. Without hesitation, he aimed and pulled the trigger straight at Hope's head.

But Chase was there, blocking the shot again. This time, though, he was furious. He whipped the bullets back at Jack with fierce force, striking his face with silver-dollar-sized welts. His right eye began to swell shut, but Jack didn't pause.

With blood and sweat dripping from him, he made a frantic dash toward the main stairwell leading to the dungeon. He knew he had slim to no chance of surviving the battle below.

The vine slithered across the cobblestone floor, snapping at his boots as he sprinted. His adrenaline surged, and he pushed himself harder, leaping with everything he had. The pain in his left calf shot through him as it hyperextended, and he screamed, but he didn't stop.

He sailed through the air, narrowly clearing a small window in the stained glass. The top of his head, torso, and legs scraped painfully against the jagged edges as he landed.

The vine caught up to him, wrapping tightly around his boot and ankle, dragging him down as he struggled to free himself.

Then!!.. In pure desperation and with his skill set, he drew out his sword, dangling in mid-air!! Lancing off that pesky part of the plant!! He takes a hard, fast head over his shoulders, then tumbles down the stairs; he controls it as much as possible, turning it into a tight tucked, ninja roll!!.. Jack stood up, taking a lot of damage, leaning on his gold handrail… huffing and puffing. His adrenaline aggressively about, coursing through his veins!!.. About the only thing keeping him going!!.. At this point, He is more mentally worn out!!.. Not quite, catching his breath, the Vine then rips the rail and bolts out of the stone wall!!. Jack nearly fell over!!.. He then looked up at the window he had just leaped through; the relentless plant rapidly descended straight at his head, Jack just ducking, deaking, bobbing, and weaving out of the way!!! My home!! He shouts!!.. Glancing down the stairs, watching the Vine engulfing the ceiling. He then scurried down the stairs.

He began to make his way down the main hallway. That plant now has a solid foothold and is growing on the whole estate! Hope then makes her way back into her body. Thank you, my king, you gave me that invincible shield!!, kissing him on his cheek. Okay, I can see Jack. He is trapped, heading towards a dead end!!.. There is also a man named Medaling Madaliss!!.. He will be no match; go to him straight after. Let's go finish this!!! I bet the Vine will beat us to it!!.. Okay, everyone, be extra careful he is hurt, cornered, in his home, with guns, grenades, knives… let's be extra crafty, stealthy… GOD, bless. Then Miles and Faith's ears perked up. They turned towards an oak door. Do you hear that? Asked Miles; Faith nodded yes. They zoned in on the pattern of Jack's boots running!!

Heavy breathing…you bet that's Jack, said Hope. I see him and Ozzy and others. They are okay. Mider let out a howl!!!! Then, the wolves of the squad joined in a celebration howl!!!! Hope waited for them to finish. Then said. I can also see all the guards that we put under the bed. They are all wrapped up in the Vines. As are the ones in the yard and rooftop!!.. They sure mean business, said Miles… Chase snickers… he then uses his mind powers to release the lock hold on the doors and then opens them. The hallway is filled with statues, battle armor, expensive oil paintings, and many more deer. Lion… heads on the walls. Handmade furniture everywhere. Miles said I bet all of this stuff is stolen!!.. Hope nodded yes. Then she said that would be a safe bet!!.. Still, no one is on site. Miles… I can smell fear, as can I, said Faith!!.. Mider let out a huge bark!!.. Miles.. Do you see that? He is looking at a blood droplet trail. All eyes light up with excitement!! Start from scratch. All knowing the thrill of the hunt!!.. Mider and the wolves are licking their chops with authority!!.. Dripping drool all over the white marble floor. Others grinding their fangs!!.. Mider and his wolf pals are like kids at Christmas… souls lighting up!!. The hairs standing up from the back of the neck all down the spine. Tails fluffed and puffed up!! Miles asks them. Let's do this traditional, old-school. Chase nodded yes; then Hope said yes. Chase and I will only use our powers if needed, not wanted!!.. Needed!!.. That's a different fish to fry!!.. Everyone looked at one another, nodding yes!!.. Miles then ran over to the red dropped splatters, sticking his snout an inch above it. Then, inhaling in a big whiff of the scent. He looked over at them with a confident, smirky smile. Like I said, I can smell fear!!.. And evil, a great adversary. Meaning a worthy opponent!!.. Cornered, scared, hurt. Almost in full desperation mode!!.. In his home!! Lock, stock, and barrel!! Miles... I can see 38 caliber bullets he dropped, reloading, that he probably keeps on his ankle. The blood trail goes much further than I can see, said Miles. Scoops the hawk, then lands on Miles' shoulder, then says not only can I see where the blood trail ends, but I can also see a few traps he set!!.. Do tell said, Chase!?.. Well, he is quite sophisticated. He has a few booby traps set, also a couple bear traps set!!.. Behind the tiger and wolverine statues. Did you all hear that? Asked Hope!?.. Because if need be, I can see further than that. All locking eyes then nodding yes. Hope said good; please be mindful of what you can see, hear and feel. I can assist in all the above in a heartbeat. Hope looking at all the angels being helpful. Safety first and all that great stuff!! Moving forward, Chase spoke; please take cover from what we can. Nothing over fancy. The right spot to get the job done! Just being resourceful when push comes to shove, doing what needs to be done!!.. Being mindful of each and every one of your lives really is!!.. Forever and ever!! Let's do this!!.. Shouted Faith!!! Her strong and somewhat silent type had taken a back seat!!.. She pounced on top of a lion statue! Too much talk!!.. Talk is cheap!! We are all blessed with being doers, not running our mouths. But our freedom of speech. Our self and family values… and beyond!!.. Long story short, we have our prey cornered.

"Do it in peace, or whatever it takes!" they all whispered. She pounced from one statue to the next, and Miles and the others followed in her paw prints, gradually forming their own hunting paths. Miles and Faith took turns leading, both sniffing the blood trail. They froze when they spotted a large black soldier's boot peeking out from behind a fancy saltwater fish tank with a solid base stand. The boot's toe was the only part visible, while the fish swam around calmly, unaware of anything out of the ordinary. Through the glass, the only thing visible beyond the tank was a wall with an oil painting of a leopard.

They stood still, waiting patiently. Miles whispered, "I can't see the blood trail beyond that point."

"Nor I," said the hawk.

Faith whispered, "I think it's a decoy."

Scoops, perched on Faith's shoulder, fluttered his wings twice and flew up to the top of the fish tank. Slowly, he peered over the edge, looking down the glass side. Faith was right—it was just a pair of boots. The bird's eyes confirmed it was a fake-out, a diversion.

They moved ahead cautiously, sniffing and peering around corners. Suddenly, they stopped in their tracks, staring at a stained glass window depicting an elephant. Hope, who knew all, stayed silent.

Crack!! Smash!! Glass shattered everywhere as Ozzy leaped in. Wrecker, Wisdom, and Whiskey followed close behind, with the rest of the crew soon in tow—Soul and Skye among them. Without missing a beat, Ozzy barked, "Birds, go ahead! Report back ASAP." The birds of prey soared off.

Miles grinned. "Well, hi to you too, Ozzy. Perfect entrance!"

The bear growled in agreement.

"It's been a while since we've had to do a quest together. I miss it," Ozzy said, as the giant Kodiak sauntered down the blood trail.

The drops were larger now. After a few more steps, they could see where Jack had changed his bandage and two more bleeding points, forming a faint set of blood trails.

"He's a real fighter… but on the wrong side," Miles muttered.

Ozzy smiled, then grinned wider. "Only fifty feet to the end of the last room. The vines have everything blocked and tackled that we didn't already take care of. Feisty fellows. A true Godsend. They're on the good side, the pure white light side!"

# Chapter 14

Let's get this dirtbag first!!.. Wisdom flicked that red and white super fluffy tail again, that flashy fellow!!.. Whiskey then leaped off Miles, bounced off Ozzy, and landed on an elephant statue scurrying up the tusk, the trunk. Jumped up on the head!! Rubbing his two paws together in delight. He then took out a dagger and carved a few jewels out of the stone face: diamonds, rubies, sapphires. Putting some in a camouflage Satchel, then swallowed the rest for safekeeping. Retrieve them later.

Soul, that crafty crow could always see a few steps ahead, had pecked a few jewels out with his beak. Took them and flew over the two bear traps, dropping one on each, triggering the traps shut. With no one getting hurt, using his wits was just as mighty as the pen and sword!!.., Whiskey slid down the statue and scampered over, grabbing the jewels. Miles and Faith were taking turns leading the way, back and forth, taking cover behind whatever they could!!.. Scoops flew back, landing on Ozzy... I have seen Jack. He has been keeping away from us and the vines so far by hiding in and amongst the waterfalls, rocks, and garden flowers!!.. He almost had a clean shot at me; I just got to cover before he took the shot.

Lucky then flew out of Hope's pocket, saying how lucky!! That's my department!! I did notice my jewels had an extra glow to them!!.. The ladybug then winked at the hawk. He returned the wink... Thank you, said Ozzy!! Scoops... He's behind the last statue, it's a statue of Jack!!!... Can't miss it. Ozzy, it is very valuable, but he could move, or anything is possible!! All guards up... Picking up more momentum, the squad of creatures moving faster and faster!!.. Only twenty feet from the spot where he was last seen. The mighty vines were growing rapidly... Moving passed them, leaving them unharmed. There is a trickle, a small splash, splash, noise coming from the water.

Miles picks up on the sound of teeth biting metal… a sound he knows... A grenade pin is being pulled out!! He yells out and takes cover!!.. Get down!!.. It lands in the middle of most of them. All Chase can think of is blocking it. He then pictures a shield around them… pop!!!.. A white dome-shaped glowing light appeared. Chase, staring at it, made it brighter, thicker!!.. Boom!!!... The grenade explodes!! Metal shrapnel is going every which way. Breaking a bear statue in half!!.. The top half of it came crashing down, landing on the shield right above wisdom and whiskey!!.. Blocking them from harm!!.. The slab of stone hovers along with a bunch of metal. Stone and wood pieces… one of which is stuck right in front of jewel's face!!.. Hope said that was amazing!!..

Chase then takes out one of his grenades, throwing it straight at Jack!!.. He jumped behind a bolder... Boom!!!... Half the pond stream, rocks, and garden flew in every direction!!.. Jack was unscathed from that assault. He goes to put in a fresh magazine clip in his AK47. Skye swoops down in a dive bomb. Going for his eyes!!.. Jack quickly moved his head back at the last possible fraction of a second!!.. The eagles' talons ripping out one eye, and just missed the other!!.. Jack screams!!.. Then shoots at Skye... Clipping his wing, only nicking him... Knocking off a few feathers!!.. He then hurls yet another grenade!!.. Boom!!!... Chase, still holding up the shield. It does not penetrate... Then he takes aim and fires the gun like a Wild West madman!!.. The bullets are cutting statues in half!!.. Then sticking to the shield!! He screams in pain... Frustration!!.. Soul the crow flies over him. Jack then makes a small slip on a very slippery slope... His only eye is fully committed... Focused on the crow!! Going for the shot!!.. The gun is going up!!..up!!..up!!...

In the midst of the heated battle, a tiny window of opportunity opened. "No guts, no glory!" Miles and Faith leapt off the grandfather clock, pouncing on Jack and sending him crashing down onto the muddy marble floor. Both wolves sank their teeth into his hands, and Jack let out a blood-curdling scream. "Meadaliss!!!" he shouted.

Ozzy calmly approached and placed a paw on Jack's throat, pinning him down. "Okay, guys, just knock him out," Miles said.

Jack began flexing, squirming, trying to muscle his way out, but with a single, powerful squeeze from Ozzy's massive Kodiak bear paw, it was lights out for Jack. A collective sigh of relief echoed around them, while some of the group reveled in the adrenaline of the hunt, craving more of the intense rush.

With Jack subdued, they quickly tied him up and gagged him, ensuring he couldn't escape.Chase then released the force field around them and made one around Jack. He's coming with us!! Let's finish this place off!!.. All started running towards the basement stairs... Jack hovers beside Chase, going wherever he goes. Reaching the top of the stone steps. Vines come from every which way... Now, all the crew could hear snoring!!.. Deep snoring!!.. Then, help me!!.. It's a soft-spoken lady's voice!!.. Miles peers one eye and ear around the corner; at the bottom, it's a goose in a cage. Others in cages, too!!.. He then looked over to see where the snore fest was coming from... Hard to tell... The vines had beaten them to it. Just a silhouette of a human with a mouth sticking out!!.. Miles, then giving the green light, go ahead. All then enter the room. The vine is hard at work to get the cages open. Chase spoke up, let me help, friends. He then made short work of the locks, busting them off!!

The goose flew out on the loose!!.. It's Carole!!!.., Miles' mum!!.. And that's Daniel, the lemur, said Carole, and that's Shelly, the horseshoe crab. The other four, we don't know. All of them are from the same island; she then turned into her wolf form... Some of the creatures are passed out. Hope... No worries, we will fix them up. Miles gave his mum a hug. " Mum, mum, we are on a quest to make things good and right; proud of you guys!!

Jewels then came down to Carole. Then Miles got on the radio to stampers and perogy on the boat. Okay, it's all clear here; please come get our Atlas statue, bring it back to the boat, and hurry!!!... Stampers, Heath, and Maximus are all on the same radio channel, and all cheered Hurray!!!... Nice work, said Heath!!.. Then Tuffy barked with delight mider, and the wolves had a howl, too!! But not Allie!!.. Some huffing and puffing came from the stairs… the gorgeous wolf then emerged. Miles asked, "Are you okay!?".. I've been waiting to tell you, Miles. You're going to have another son or daughter!!! Faith will be a big sister!!! All teared up!!! Miles letting loose a huge happy howl!!!... Then, hugged Allie; Hope and Chase both said that's wonderful!!.. Congratulations!! At the same time!!.. Hope.. Do you two want to know if it's a boy or a girl!!.. Both Allie and Miles nodded yes.

Hope, it's a happy, healthy baby girl!!. All cheered!!! Hope then said, and very soon, your son will come!! All cheered again!! Miles spoke up; we will name our newest family member, Kinsey, for the girl!!... And Kayser for the boy!! Allie smiled and then said I love those names!! Miles then asked Gunner do you four want to come with the rest of us back to your new home. Or stay here for now? Gunner said let's put Jack and all these evil men in the cages!!.. Give them a taste of their own medicine!!.. Besides, they do not deserve to be free to do what they want... All agreed. Yes, they stay here for now said Miles. At least give them a chance to cleanse themselves up. And if not, jail is the only option. Gunner.. We will stay here to watch and guard them. Mighty generous of you four loyal, lovely guys!! You are welcome on our island anytime. We will leave you one of the boats and all the food and drinks.

"Mider here will teach you how to operate the boat," Miles announced. "Before we leave, we'll load it with food, seeds for crops, and supplies. Make sure the radios are in perfect working order so we can stay in touch."

Gunner's foursome saluted their fellow soldiers, a silent acknowledgment of their shared mission. Miles then turned to the group. "Okay, everyone, help gather the men from the rooftop and the yard. Bring them down here and lock them up."

Most of the team stayed behind to round them up. As they walked up the stairs, Hope glanced around and asked, "Does it feel different here to you?"

Everyone agreed. The once oppressive tension had lifted, replaced by a sense of peace and renewal. When they reached the courtyard, the difference was striking—it looked and felt transformed.

Miles noticed Faith off to the side, scanning a clover patch. She leaned down, plucked a four clover with her fangs, and grinned. "Dad! I found another one!"

She held it up proudly. "Do you want it?"

Miles smiled. "No, thank you, my angel. Remember, the magic belongs to the one who finds it."

Faith beamed, tucking the clover away. Meanwhile, the others worked quickly, bringing the prisoners down to the basement.

Stampers, following the peanut trail left behind, reached the statue. With a mighty crash, the front iron gates crumbled. The massive elephant wrapped his trunk around the stone-shaped Atlas, lifted it, and began carrying it back to the boat.

With all the prisoners now locked in cages, Miles turned to the vines. "I'm sure our friends here will help keep watch."

Chase used his power to weld the bars shut, sealing their fate.

Just then, Jack stirred, groaning as he regained consciousness. He clutched the empty space where his eye had been, mirroring the captain, both of them writhing in pain.

Chase untied them and removed their gags.

Silence.

Neither man spoke a word..

All of the Kozoways, jewels glowed!!.. Then, a feeling of love cast over them. God's Rainbow came down to both the wounded men!!.. A white flash came from both their faces!!.. Then disappeared with the rainbow!!.. My eyes!! And my eye!!.. I can see it again!!.. I have eyes again!!.. As did Jack.. It seems as though God wanted to show some of his powers, even to these dirtbags!!.. Everyone stood in true awe!!!... Miles said let that be a start to a lesson for you both!!.. He has decided to be kind and give you both healing mercy. Instead of throwing lightning bolts at you two!!.. And all the evil men here!!.. How disgraceful!!.. All the bad, right down, evil things you men have done with your miserable lives!! How dare you!!!...

Gunner, you're in charge around here now. We will stay in constant contact!! Thank you, said Gunner, no thank you, said Miles. As they made their way to the boats, Mider said to keep up, Gunner, let's get there! You will be a veteran boat captain in no time, brother!!.. Gunner barked in joy!!.. On their way, they couldn't help but notice all the new wildlife flourishing!!!... Everywhere!!!... And the beach now has families of crabs playing and the big blue lady now had many schools of fish, swimming all around the boats!!..

The island is now restored, filled with new, positive roots, land, air, and sea... Life's good!!!... All arrived and gave Stampers a hand with the statue. Then, unload all the food, drinks, and supplies they have with them on the beach. Miles then picked up the radio... Heath, come in!!... Heath hears!! What's going on, little buddy!? Miles... Life's good!!!.. Big buddy!!!... Glad to hear, said Heath!!!... What can I do for you!? We are about to cruise over the sea, we are coming home!!.. How about you cook up one of your world-famous feasts for all of us!! I'm already on it!!

O, thank goodness I'm starving!!.. Said, Ozzy!!.. That makes all of us, said Miles!!!... Allie gave Miles a kiss on the cheek; Hope did the same to Chase. Allie then took Miles's paw and put it on her tummy. Can you feel what she said!? Yes!! That's little Kinsey moving!!!... Carole and Faith both came over to have a feel of the baby kicking and a family hug!! Miles said I can't wait to be home sweet home and feast!! Thorn, Lola, and Mc. Maddy all joined up with the rest of the Kozoways; Gunner sure does have the skill set to man the boat; both he and Mider bark with joy!!..

Doing eternity….Figure eights and heart shapes with the boat. The three birds of prey celebrate in the breathtaking blue sky with some friendly play fighting with each other, the sun shining down on everyone. All have also gone back to normal on the red-sanded island, same back home on Kozoway Island, and everything is flourishing!!.. Even Cornell... Miles's dad had come down from the castle to the beach to enjoy the perfect sunny day. He had not been feeling well... Now... Better than ever! !... Hope tells the family the amazing news!!.. They all trade warm hugs, with the four dogs staying behind. Said they will see you soon…. To one another.

Miles gave the order to pull anchor. Chase fired up the engines, the steady hum blending with the rhythmic crash of the waves. As the boat began to move, Miles set the mood, turning on the stereo and letting Johnny Cash's deep, soulful voice fill the air.

With a final glance at the island, they watched as it grew smaller on the horizon. The four loyal dogs stood at the edge of the deck, ears perked, eyes fixed on the fading shore. The squads waved back and forth, their hearts overflowing with a sense of victory and love—life, once tainted by darkness, was pure again.

Yet, they all knew their mission wasn't over. There was still more to set right. But they faced the future with unshakable faith, filled with the purest confidence in God's love.

As the vessel cruised forward, embraced by the golden glow of the tropical sun, the Kozoways stood together, ready for whatever lay ahead. Peace, purpose, and the divine surrounded them— guiding their path in the name of Jesus, the source of all that is good and pure.

## THE END